Marry her? He w...

Cammy sank back, shaken, her eyes never leaving Adam's face. Was he joking?

"Well, Cammy?" he asked.

She tipped her head back and looked up at him. Usually she *liked* to look at him, but the grimly stubborn set to his chin and the determination glinting in his eyes worried her. Too much had happened in the past twenty-four hours—in the two months since Gran died, really—and Cammy wasn't sure she could cope just now with whatever was on Adam's mind.

"I'm tired," she said. "Can this possibly wait until tomorrow?"

"No it can't," he denied flatly. And then, in the least romantic tone imaginable he said, "How about it, Cammy? Will you marry me?"

Dear Reader,

May...the month when flowers—and love—are in full bloom—especially here at Silhouette Romance. And as you know, spring is also that special time of year when a man's thoughts turn to love. Be they the boy next door or a handsome, mysterious stranger, our heroes are no exception! Six lucky heroines are about to find their dreams of happy-ever-after come true as once again, Silhouette Romance sweeps you away with heartwarming, poignant stories of love.

In the months to come, we'll be publishing romances by many of your all-time favorites, including Diana Palmer, Brittany Young and Annette Broadrick. And coming next month, Nora Roberts will launch her not-to-be-missed Calhoun Women Series with the June Silhouette Romance, *Courting Catherine.*

WRITTEN IN THE STARS is a very special event for 1991. Each month, we're proud to present a Silhouette Romance that focuses on the hero—and his astrological sign. May features the stubborn-but-loveable Taurus man. Our authors and editors have created this delightfully romantic series especially for you, the reader, and we'd love to hear what you think. After all, at Silhouette Romance, we take our readers' comments to heart!

Please write to us at Silhouette Romance
300 East 42nd Street
New York, New York
10017

We look forward to hearing from you!

Sincerely,

Valerie Susan Hayward
Senior Editor

MARCY GRAY

Be My Wife

Silhouette *Romance*

Published by Silhouette Books New York

America's Publisher of Contemporary Romance

SILHOUETTE BOOKS
300 E. 42nd St., New York, N.Y. 10017

BE MY WIFE

ISBN: 0-373-08792-6

First Silhouette Books printing May 1991

Printed in the U.S.A.

MARCY GRAY

has always loved reading romances and can't resist a story that makes her cry. Though she has been writing romances for ten years, she looks for story ideas in everyday life, and spends hours just watching people to help develop her characters. Her love of travel enables her to research her books.

Chapter One

"Great news, Cammy! We've got a buyer for the farm."

Camelia Anderson calmly pushed the plate of oatmeal-raisin cookies across the table to her cousin as if he hadn't spoken. "Help yourself, Lance. I took these out of the oven just before you drove up."

Lance's forehead puckered. "Didn't you hear what I said? I've found someone who wants to buy this place, lock, stock, and barrel."

Cammy selected one of the chewy treats and took a small bite, then realized it was no use trying to ignore Lance's announcement. She'd never known him to give up once he got an idea in his head, and he'd been harping on variations of this subject for a month now.

Her appetite deserting her, she put the uneaten portion of cookie down on her napkin and lifted serious eyes to the man sitting across from her. "I don't want to sell the farm. It's been in the family forever, and besides, Gran's only been gone six weeks. It's too soon."

"I know you miss her," he said with a nod, and in response, an almost unbearable ache filled her throat. Lord, yes, she missed her grandmother!

Looking sympathetic, Lance continued. "Well, shoot, honey, we all do. But life has to go on. We sure can't afford to lose this sale because of some kind of silly sentimentality over the old home place. I'm counting on my share of the money to start a college fund for the kids, and Joe Kenneth and Babette both have plenty of uses for their part. With the real estate market being what it is these days, we're lucky anybody's interested enough to make an offer. Like I told Monica, it's a good thing Billy Crenshaw wants to expand his farm operation just now."

Cammy conceded silently that what he said was probably true. She had kept up with the nightly news enough to know something about the economic woes sweeping the country, affecting in particular agricultural communities like Comanche, Texas, where she lived. But that didn't change the fact that selling this place might be more than she could stand just now.

"I'm not ready to move," she repeated softly, hoping he would understand. "If Gran told me once, she must have told me a hundred times she wanted me to stay here as long as it makes me happy. That's why she left this house to me. It's my home—the only one I've ever known."

"Well, ordinarily that would be just fine, but we have to be practical. It's time you found a husband and started a family of your own, like the rest of us." Lance smiled at her in that persuasive way of his that had always gotten him what he wanted. More than ten years her senior, he'd learned long ago how to wrap her around his little finger. He was her favorite cousin, and knew it. "You're twenty-one years old, Cammy. Nobody as pretty as you are should end up an old maid."

She smiled and shrugged off his flattery. With her brown hair and heart-shaped face, Cammy considered herself plain and uninteresting, the very opposite of her attractive cousins, all of whom possessed striking blond coloring and strong personalities. "I don't think I'll ever marry, Lance."

"Sure you will. For a while there, everybody figured you'd marry Wesley Dean. I still don't know what you didn't like about him. Anyway, you need to start looking for the right man, and in order to do that, you need to get yourself a job, move into one of those new apartment buildings in Stephenville or Brownwood...maybe even Dallas."

Shaking her head, Cammy glanced around the kitchen with its out-of-date appliances and faded wallpaper, unable to imagine herself ever living anywhere but right here in this old-fashioned farmhouse where she'd grown up. "What sort of job could I get?" she asked quizzically. "Would anyone hire me to plant a garden or to can okra or peaches? To make quilts or bake for them? Or tend to old, sick folks? Because that's just about all I've ever done."

He looked irritated. "You don't have to remind me, Cammy. Believe me, we're all aware of the sacrifices you made, helping Gran take care of Grandpa until he died, and then nursing Gran herself after her heart attack."

"Oh, but that's not what I—"

Waving aside her protest that it hadn't been a sacrifice, Lance reached for a cookie and started to bite into it, then pointed it at her instead, his expression self-righteous. "That's just the problem. You've never had much of a life of your own, and it's time we did something about that. Once we sell this place, you can use your share of the money to go to beauty school, or take one of those secretarial courses they're always advertising on TV.''

''But I don't want to go to beauty school or become a secretary,'' she said reasonably.

Lance frowned as if he thought she was deliberately being difficult. ''Well, then, maybe you could start some kind of business of your own...selling all those quilts you make, for example.''

She considered that a moment. ''Maybe you're right. I'll bet I could do that right here. I wouldn't have to move in order to sell quilts.'' The longer she thought about it, the better she liked the idea. ''I could set up Gran's quilting frames in the parlor and work in there. And I could display the finished quilts around the living room—''

''Cammy, don't be ridiculous!'' Lance cut in sharply, his charm vanishing as his patience wore thin. ''You can't open a quilt shop way out here in the country. You wouldn't have any customers. And you have no business staying in this old house. It's too big for one person, you'd just rattle around all by yourself.'' His voice softened and he forced another smile. ''The whole point is to get you out among people, where you can make friends. I'm only thinking of you when I say that.''

''But I have friends—''

''Besides,'' he interrupted her firmly, ''it's essential that you sell your part of the farm, too. Mr. Crenshaw insists on buying all four hundred acres or none at all, and I know you wouldn't be so selfish as to cheat my twins out of an education. Not to mention,'' he added with a chiding look, ''prevent Babette from finishing the new house she and Grady are building, or mess up Joe Kenneth's credit rating. He's had a run of bad luck holding on to a job lately.''

Cammy sat stunned, not knowing what to say to that. She couldn't remember anybody ever accusing her of being selfish before. All her life she'd worked hard to help the people she loved, which left her, as Lance had just said, not much of a life of her own. Because her parents had died when she was a baby, Gran and Grandpa, Uncle Joe and Aunt Nettie, and her three cousins had always been everything to her. Now her cousins were all she had left, and here was her much-loved and admired Lance suggesting that Cammy was about to ruin their lives if she remained in the one place where she belonged! Didn't he realize how important home and family were to her?

"I would never hurt any of you if I could help it," she muttered.

He smiled as if her words had been exactly what he'd been waiting to hear. "Good girl!" He patted her hand with hearty approval. "I didn't really think you would if you knew what was at stake here. That's why I went ahead and made an appointment to see the lawyer first thing Monday morning about probating Gran's will, so we can get the ball rolling and complete the sale of the land. I want to take this load off your shoulders and handle things for you."

Usually when he beamed at her like that, it was as if the sun had burst out from behind a cloud, but now Cammy felt chilled inside in spite of the way Lance was trying to reassure her. "You made an appointment to see Adam Neil?" she asked. "But Gran named me executor of her will. Shouldn't I go with you to see Adam?"

"I don't want you to have to worry your pretty head about it, Cammy. Adam's secretary said you'll have to sign some papers eventually, but in the meantime I can deal with him and save you the hassle. You know how difficult and unfriendly Adam can be when he wants to." He stood up to go, taking a handful of cookies with him as he strolled to the door. "The first thing I'll probably do is hire a surveyor, so don't be concerned if you see some men working around the place.''

Cammy slowly followed him out onto the porch. He was halfway to his car when he shouted back, "Maybe you can come over to the house for Sunday dinner, honey! I'll have Monica call you.'' Then with a wave he was gone.

She turned and stared at the blue and purple, trumpet-shaped blossoms on the morning-glory vines that climbed all over the porch railing. The flowers, so fresh and open every time the sun rose, were shriveled now, all closed in on themselves as the May twilight stretched in lavender shadows across the grassy yard. That was how she felt—closed up and lonely...a bit frightened. What was she going to do? Where would she go?

The handle of the five-gallon bucket bit into the tender flesh of her arm as Cammy lugged it inside. She set the pail, heavy with squash, cucumbers, and ears of corn, on the kitchen floor and then plopped down onto one of the cane-bottom chairs and exhaled in a rush. Untying the strings of her calico bonnet, she pulled it off and tossed it over the back of another chair, shook her hair loose, and then propped both elbows on the table to rest her chin on her hands.

Mercy, but she was hot and tired! She could almost hear Gran's gentle voice now, scolding her for gathering vegetables from the garden in the heat of the day. It was fool-hardy, she knew very well, to risk heatstroke. But sometimes she just couldn't sit still. Sometimes she had to keep busy or go crazy from thinking.

It was Friday of a week that had seemed endless. Cammy had worked hard in the garden and finished up a baby quilt for one of the neighbors, and she'd had visits from the minister and several friends from church, but she couldn't talk to them about the one thing that was bothering her: Lance's insistence that she sell the farm. That was simply too private a matter. Gran had always taught her that family linen shouldn't be aired in public. As she hadn't seen any of her cousins since Lance's visit, there had been no opportunity to discuss her worries with anyone, and that last conversation with him had been weighing heavily on her mind. She kept wondering what was happening, especially when she saw the surveyors scoping out the farm on Wednesday, but Lance didn't call to enlighten her.

Neither had Monica called to invite her to dinner last Sunday. Lance had probably forgotten he'd suggested it; after all, Monica and Lance were busy, with the ten-year-old twin girls and two younger boys, and both of them working full-time. Instead, Cammy and her friend Margo went out for pizza after church. But she thought Lance could have at least reported to her on his meeting with Adam Neil!

"'Don't worry your pretty head about it,'" she quoted her eldest cousin aloud and then asked herself with a twinge of bitterness, "How am I supposed to keep from worrying?"

Just then the telephone rang in the hall, and Cammy jumped a foot. Goodness, her nerves were shot! She'd been starting like that every time the phone rang lately, fearing it would be notification that the sale of the farm had gone through and she should start packing. She hurried to snatch the receiver off the hook. "Hello."

"Cammy?"

Her heart stumbled and began banging against her ribs when she recognized the low masculine voice. "Yes?" she said warily.

"Cammy, this is Adam."

She knew very well that it was Adam, and she reacted as she used to whenever he'd called to talk business with her grandmother: she prayed fervently that she wouldn't make an utter fool of herself in front of Comanche's most intriguing resident. Adam had been educated at Harvard, in addition to being the sole surviving heir to the considerable wealth of the Neil family. The fact that he was still a bachelor at thirty-two, and that he never showed more than a fleeting interest in any of the local women, elevated him to the status of mystery man extraordinaire in the eyes of Cammy's girlfriends, and most certainly in Cammy's eyes.

Of course, there were his scars. Some folks said they accounted for his never having married, although in Cammy's considered opinion they didn't detract a bit from his dark and somewhat brooding good looks.

"Hello, Adam," she said with the cautious politeness that he seemed to bring out in her. She was always afraid of saying too much and revealing what he did to her nerves. "How are you?"

"Fine," he said dismissively, as if his health wasn't the issue here. "I've been intending to call you ever since the funeral to ask how *you* are. Unfortunately I've been out of town on business a good part of the time."

"Well . . . welcome home."

"Thanks." He added impatiently, "So—how *are* you?"

"I'm just fine." She made a wry face into the mirror that hung on the wall over the telephone stand, wishing she dared to ask how he expected her to be in view of the fact that she was about to lose her home.

"Good. I'm glad to hear that." He sounded sincere, if preoccupied, and she knew he probably meant what he said. Adam might be a sophisticated local celebrity and something of an unpredictable loner, but he was also above all else a forthright man. Gran had admired him prodigiously. She used to tease Cammy, suggesting that of all the men in town, Adam Neil was by far the best husband material—

Never mind Gran's teasing, Cammy warned herself sharply and jerked her attention back to the conversation.

"I've been expecting to hear from you all week . . . ever since I saw Lance on Monday," Adam was saying.

Cammy's heart rate accelerated, and this time Adam's fascinating appeal was the last thing on her mind. "Do you mean you've already got the papers ready for me to sign?"

He hesitated, then grunted. "Look, Cammy, I need to talk to you," he said without answering her question. "Would it be convenient for me to drop by your house in a few minutes?"

Oh, terrific! In a few minutes she was going to have her world shattered!

Cammy stared at the dial of the old black telephone. Gran and Grandpa had had this phone installed before Cammy was even born. It was a wonder the thing still worked, she thought irrelevantly.

"Cammy?" Adam repeated. "Would that be convenient?"

She cleared her throat. "Well, you see, Adam, I've, uh, just come in from working in the garden and I'm a . . . I'm an awful mess. Maybe it would be better if you came another time. Another day." *Another year,* she thought wildly.

His voice was quiet but resolute. "I think I'd better see you as soon as possible."

"But I'm so dirty—"

"Cammy," he cut in, with a dry self-mocking humor that she'd never heard from him before, "I can guarantee that no matter how dirty and messy you are, you'll still look better than I do. But take a shower if it'll make you feel better. I'll be there in an hour.'' And he hung up before she could say another word.

Exactly an hour later she watched an expensive gray car pull to a stop beneath one of the huge pecan trees that shaded the yard, and Adam got out from behind the steering wheel. She wondered where his briefcase was as he strode up onto the porch empty-handed.

Cammy had shampooed her hair in the tub, there being no shower in the antiquated bathroom. Then she'd blown it dry with the hair dryer her cousin Babette had given her for Christmas one year, wishing as she did so that she knew how to make the most of its gentle natural curl. For a moment she'd even debated trying some of the odd bits of makeup that she'd bought from time to time, but she was afraid she'd end up looking like a clown. She settled for applying a touch of lipstick that matched the delicate pink dress she'd decided to wear—her best Sunday dress, purchased on a shopping expedition to Brownwood before Gran got sick. Everyone said the dress was perfect on her. Cammy admitted that she did rather like the way she looked in it, with its slender waist and full skirt.

She didn't dare ask herself why she was getting so gussied up. But a suspicion lurked in the shadows at the back of her mind, and when Adam stepped into the kitchen and spoke her name in husky greeting, she couldn't deny the tiny starburst of pleasure that exploded inside her.

She couldn't deny it, but she absolutely refused to let herself pay any attention to the tingling warmth spinning through her. Was she crazy? Adam Neil wouldn't look twice at Camelia Anderson!

Motioning to the table, she said, ''Will you sit down, Adam?'' As he passed her, she drew a deep shaky breath and inhaled a whiff of his mysteriously seductive scent.

Lawsy mercy! If every man wore Adam's after-shave, womankind would probably complain of far fewer headaches at bedtime. Not that Cammy had any experience of headaches at bedtime, but she'd heard jokes....

Disciplining her thoughts, she told herself he looked a hundred times better than she. Even scarred. Even though she'd spent the past hour working nonstop to improve herself. Tailored to fit his lean, six-feet-tall frame, Adam's white summer suit and pale blue shirt were the last word in traditional Southern elegance, and his black hair was cut short in a style that showed off his beautifully shaped head.

Despite having known him all her life, Cammy had never figured out if he sported a deep, perpetual tan or if his skin was just naturally that swarthy olive tone. She never saw him in anything except very proper suits with long-sleeved shirts that remained forever buttoned at collar and cuffs. The backs of his hands and the left side of his face bore faint, faded scars from some terrible burns that he'd suffered long ago...scars that were only mentioned in whispers around town. Sometimes, like today, they were barely noticeable, but other days they either showed up starkly white against his dark coloring, or unusually flushed and angry looking. Rumor had it that his clothes hid more scars.

Staring at him, Cammy wondered if Adam had any idea that she had tried more than once to imagine him without clothes on. Wouldn't Gran have been shocked!

"You lied to me," she muttered.

He looked startled. "I beg your pardon?"

Embarrassed by her wayward thoughts and unwilling to remind him that he'd promised she would look better than he, Cammy turned her back and hurried to fix two glasses of iced tea. A minute later she set them on the table along with a pound cake she'd baked that morning. "Never mind," she said brightly. "Have something to eat."

He let her serve him a piece of cake and dutifully took a bite, then put down his fork and touched his napkin to his mouth as if preparing to say something. When she met his gray eyes, she was surprised to see a whole storm of worry in them. "I've been waiting for you to call, Cammy. Why haven't you?"

"Was I supposed to call you?" she asked, feeling definitely off balance.

"You *are* the executor of Miss Louella's estate, aren't you?" Of course he knew she was, since he'd drawn up the will after her grandfather died.

"Yes, but Lance is handling things."

He closed his mouth tightly as if he disapproved, then asked in a deceptively calm voice, "Do you mind telling me whose idea that was?"

"Well, Lance suggested it." She frowned, twisting her hands together. "You did say he saw you on Monday."

He nodded shortly. "Haven't you talked to Lance since then? Didn't he give you my message?"

Her stomach was starting to feel uneasy. "What message?"

"He didn't tell you." Adam stood up and flattened both palms on the table, then leaned toward her. His voice was quiet yet unmistakably angry. His eyes were glittering, and the scarred side of his face had suddenly gone very pale. "He went ahead and hired a surveyor, didn't he? I heard someone talking about it this morning at the café. And he didn't give you my message."

"What message?" she asked again, not sure she wanted to hear what could make the usually imperturbable Adam Neil look like that.

"I told him I wanted to see you about probating your grandmother's will. I won't deal with anyone but you."

"But . . . but why?" she asked, confused.

"Because," he said harshly, "I refuse to stand back and watch while your own family cheats you out of your home."

Chapter Two

Wasn't there an old saying that fit this occasion? Something about blood being thicker than water?

Her indignation pumping her full of courage, Cammy popped to her feet and faced Adam Neil. "Hold it just a minute! What do you mean, my family is trying to cheat me? They wouldn't do that!"

"Like hell! They've taken advantage of you all your life." He correctly read the shock in her expression and straightened up to rake a hand through his smooth dark hair in frustration. "You can't see it, though, can you?" He turned away in apparent disgust.

"There's nothing to see. We're family." To Cammy it was as simple as that.

Adam made a snorting sound, then turned back. "Haven't you read your Bible, Cammy? Brothers have been out to get each other ever since Cain killed Abel. Cousins are no different."

His reference to Cain and Abel almost threw her off track, reminding her of all manner of hushed speculation she'd overheard a long time ago about what had happened to Adam's own brother Colby...and what had caused Adam's scars. But she shoved aside the questions and said, "Not in *my* family. We love each other."

"If Lance loved you so much, why did he make sure you didn't get a chance to talk to me about your grandmother's will? Is it possible he didn't want anyone to remind you that Miss Louella arranged a life estate for you, which entitles you to the income from the farm until you decide to sell it? Could he have hoped you'd never find out that he can't legally force you to sell?"

Cammy had never understood all the details of Gran's will, nor had she been particularly interested. She would have preferred for Gran simply never to die. Besides, showing too much curiosity about what she would inherit struck her as the height of greed and ill manners.

Stoutly she said, "Lance would never force me to do anything I didn't want to do." She ignored the little voice inside that reminded her Lance wasn't above sweet-talking, not to mention out-and-out arm-twisting at times. "He's only thinking of what's best for me. That's why he went to see you in the first place."

"Lance Anderson is thinking about what's best for Lance Anderson...as usual. It's to his advantage to convince you to sell, and the sooner the better. He doesn't want to have to wait for his money."

Life had made Adam very bitter and mistrustful, Cammy thought in another abrupt shifting of her attention. She always found it impossible to think in a straight, logical line when he was around. Her gaze rested soft and troubled on his taut-skinned, hard-boned features as she mumbled more to herself than to him, "Lance said you enjoy being difficult, but I think you're just trying to live up to your reputation as a cynic."

He shrugged. "I suppose you could say I enjoy being difficult, if by that you mean I'm not willing to set aside my conscience to please Lance. And believe me, from what I've seen of it, cynicism is the only view of mankind that makes any sense."

Horrified by the realization of what she had just blurted, she could only stare at him with stricken eyes and try to apologize. "Did I say Lance called you difficult? That's not what I meant—"

The unscarred corner of his mouth curved up in a smile that wasn't reflected in his eyes—a very cynical smile. "Don't worry about it, Cammy. Your cousin has never made any secret of the fact that he considers me twisted and antisocial. We aren't the best of friends."

"Well, maybe that could change," she suggested, a sharp twinge of pain shooting through her heart at the thought of how alone Adam was... how alone he'd been almost as far back as she could remember, ever since his mother died while he was still in law school. "If you two would just sit down and have a talk—"

"We had a talk on Monday," Adam cut in. "I refused to go along with his plans to manipulate you, nor would I turn over to him the original of your grandmother's will. When he understood my position and realized that I wasn't going to change my mind, he left my office, went straight across the street, and hired George Biggs to do what he had tried to get me to do."

"George Biggs!" Cammy's blue eyes widened and she forgot her concern for Adam. "He's nothing but a shyster! Gran wouldn't have trusted him to gather the eggs, much less handle her legal business."

"No kidding?" The irony was heavy in Adam's voice.

Gulping, Cammy took refuge in denial. "I don't believe you! Lance wouldn't have hired George Biggs."

After a frozen, ten-second silence, Adam said, "That's fine. You don't have to believe me."

Something in his voice made her really look at him, and she saw that his eyes were suddenly shuttered, locked up against her. Cammy's tender heart flipped over. Could her doubting words actually have hurt him?

Before she could try to rectify any damage she might have inflicted, he was saying, "The news is all over town, but you don't have to believe that either." His voice turned wry. "Heaven knows it wouldn't be the first time local gossips were wrong." Looking tired and not very happy about the discussion, he pushed back one side of his suit coat and jammed his fist onto his hip. "Do you still have your grandmother's copy of her will, or did your cousin con you out of it?"

Cammy's flushed face provided his answer. "Lance asked to see the will right after she died."

His sensually shaped mouth thinned and tightened at the corners. "If I give you the original, will you at least do yourself the favor of taking it to an attorney who isn't under investigation by the bar for ethics violations? There's more than one decent lawyer listed in the telephone book, you know. Get one of them to go over the provisions with you and explain the safeguards your grandmother put in to protect you." He reached into the inside breast pocket of his suit and removed a folded document, which he slapped down onto the table between them so she could read the words Last Will And Testament Of Louella Anderson that were typed on the cover.

"For your own sake, Cammy, get some advice from an impartial expert before you let your family and George

Biggs screw you to the wall.'' Without even saying good-bye, he turned and left.

The noontime sun was sweltering hot, causing heat vapors to drift upward along with dust from the sidewalk as Cammy emerged from the bank in Stephenville. She got into her grandmother's old Rambler station wagon, her thoughts whirling as she tried to consider her situation calmly.

The moment Adam had left last Friday afternoon, she'd dialed Lance at work, only to discover he couldn't come to the telephone. Impatient for answers, she called George Biggs's office and identified herself to the secretary, saying, "This is in reference to my grandmother's will."

Although she crossed her fingers and hoped to be told that this was the first they'd heard of Louella Anderson's will, instead the cheerful and talkative young lady assured Cammy that Mr. Biggs had been working on it all week. "I'm pretty sure you don't have to do a thing until the day you go to probate court. The papers for the sale of the farm to Mr. Crenshaw should be ready about the same time. Your cousin is so anxious for everything to go off without a hitch, he phones every day to check on the progress."

Cammy had managed little more than a hoarse "I see" before hanging up. Then she'd called an attorney in Stephenville and scheduled the earliest available consultation appointment to do what Adam had suggested. And what she'd learned from that lawyer today had shattered the last of her illusions.

Lance really *was* trying to railroad her! It made her feel sick inside, but she couldn't deny it any longer. Not after hearing what Sam Dillby had said to her ten minutes ago: "Only a fourth of the land will actually pass to you, with the rest going in equal shares to your cousins, but the way the will is written, nobody can sell any part of the land out from under you. You have the right to benefit from any income generated by your grandparents' farm for the rest of your life, whether by leasing out the land for agricultural purposes, leasing it to a petroleum company looking for oil, farming it yourself, or whatever. Of course, at any point you can decide to sell the place and divide the money with your cousins, but...have you ever worked? Aside from helping on the farm, that is?"

Cammy shook her head. "My grandfather died while I was in high school, and soon after that Gran had her first heart attack and needed me to look after her. Anyway, there wasn't much time left for a job even after I graduated, what with tending to Gran and the house and garden."

The older man nodded kindly. "I grew up on a farm, so I know what you mean." He pursed his lips. "So you have no training and no experience, no prospects for supporting yourself anytime soon. With that in mind, you should be aware that once you decide to sell, you'll be forfeiting your life estate...not a very smart move for you to make at this point. From what you've told me of your cousin's recent actions," Mr. Dillby had concluded, "I'd say he almost succeeded in coercing you into doing something that would be to your complete disadvantage—something your grandmother evidently didn't want you to have to do, judging from the way the will reads."

So, she thought now, slumping behind the steering wheel, Adam Neil had been telling her the truth about Lance. Remorseful, Cammy remembered how she had all but accused him of lying.

A dark and brooding image of Adam arose in her mind, so vivid it startled her at first. Then she realized she had been absently rubbing the thick, crisp copy of Gran's will against her cheek and inhaling the musky male fragrance that lingered on the papers. Even though three days had passed since he'd handled them, there was no mistaking Adam's appealing scent. Suddenly Cammy found herself desperately wishing she could talk to him, and mentally blasting herself for not having trusted him more the last time they talked.

"You're a lucky young lady," Mr. Dillby had said in parting. "If that friend you mentioned hadn't warned you to look into your legal rights, you might have ended up out in the cold, despite the fact that your grandmother and the lawyer who wrote this will for her did their best to protect you."

Out in the cold, indeed! The thought of how close she had come to giving up her home made her shiver in spite of the heat.

Squaring her shoulders, Cammy resolutely started her car's engine as she asked herself if she could really count Adam Neil a friend after the other day. She wouldn't blame him if he'd washed his hands of her. Maybe she should have taken Mr. Dillby up on his offer to represent her. But Lord help her, she didn't want Mr. Dillby—she wanted Adam!

She sighed deeply, knowing she was going to have to swallow her pride and ask him to forgive her. The minute she got back to Comanche. Well, maybe not the exact minute. Maybe she could wait until tomorrow.

And then, she thought gloomily, she would have to confront Lance.

Cammy almost took the coward's way out and dealt with Adam over the telephone, but on Tuesday morning she donned her second-best dress and went to his office.

Adam sat back in his black leather chair and listened without comment to her apology, his half-flawed yet somehow wholly beautiful face revealing nothing of what he was thinking. Inside she was shaken by his judgelike silence, but when she asked if he would resume handling the affairs of her grandmother's estate, he met her gaze and, after what seemed like an eternity, nodded. "Shall I inform your cousin that I'm taking over?" he asked.

She wanted to let him, but Cammy figured she'd better start standing on her own two feet. It would be so easy to fall into the trap of depending on Adam to fight her battles, but he wouldn't always be there for her. No longer could she feel sorry for him because he was completely alone; in fact, she might just as well get used to the idea that from now on she, too, was in this thing all by herself.

"Thanks, but I'll tell him," she said, not realizing how grim she sounded.

Once at home, she left a message with the switchboard in Lance's office, asking him to stop by the farm after work, and he arrived several hours later full of concern. "Is anything wrong, Cammy? You don't usually call me at the store."

"Could you sit down and have a piece of lemon meringue pie?" To keep her hands occupied, she'd spent the afternoon baking.

"No, thanks. I don't have time. Monica will have supper ready when I get home." He stood looking at her expectantly. "What did you need to see me about?"

"I wanted to tell you—" oh, Lord, this was hard! Cammy took a deep breath and plunged on "—that I'm not ready to sell the farm."

Lance smiled as if there had to be some mistake. "Come on, Cammy, sure you are! We talked about this last week and agreed that selling would be the best thing."

"I know we talked about it, but we didn't agree. That is, I didn't agree." She got the words out in a rush. "And now that I've talked to my attorney, I understand that it would be a mistake for me to sell now."

He blinked, lines of displeasure and wary suspicion starting to groove his face. "Your attorney?"

"Adam Neil," she said.

"Adam Neil?" Lance kept his voice level with obvious effort. "I'm afraid I forgot to tell you that I hired another attorney to probate the will and help us dispose of the farm. Neil's services won't be needed."

"I know. You hired George Biggs. And of course you can retain him if you like. But as for Gran and me—" she swallowed "—well, she hired Adam as her attorney the day he started his practice here in town, and that's good enough for me. I plan to do as he advises me, and he tells me I shouldn't sell right now. You'll have to tell Mr. Crenshaw the deal is off."

"Do you mean to say you're going to listen to Adam Neil over your own cousin!"

Cammy would have done anything—well, almost anything—to wipe away that look of cold censure that was so out of place on his usually good-natured face. "He *is* my attorney, Lance, and he's been very kind about helping me."

"I can tell!" Clenching his jaw, Lance planted his legs apart and tried to stare her down. His blue eyes snapped with anger. "Cammy, you may not need the money, but the rest of us do. You can't do this to us."

Not need the money! Did he realize what he was saying? "I'm sorry, Lance, but I can do this. I *have* to. Adam tells me this is what Gran intended all along—that I'd have a place to live and some income from leasing the farm while I look for a job or go to school, since I wasn't able to work and take care of her at the same time.''

"I thought you didn't expect any thanks for that," he said sarcastically.

"I don't. But I have to pay the bills somehow."

"What about the rest of us?" His handsome mouth was etched with bitterness. "It doesn't sound as if Gran gave much thought to our needs."

"You all have jobs. You had parents to see that you were started on your careers before they died. And you have families." She reached out to him, silently asking for his understanding, but he ignored the gesture. "I promise you, Lance, as soon as I can support myself, I'll give up my life estate on the farm and let you do whatever you like with your part. You and Joe Kenneth and Babette can sell then and benefit from your share of the money, although I'll probably keep the house and enough land for my garden—"

"If you divide the place up, Billy Crenshaw won't buy it," he snapped, scowling more like a thwarted, petulant five-year-old than a thirty-two-year-old appliance salesman. "He wants it all or nothing."

"Maybe there'll be another buyer for your part."

He laughed harshly. "Don't bet on it."

She felt guilty. "I'm sorry if that's true, really I am. But Adam says this is what Gran wanted me to do."

"To hell with Adam Neil! That disfigured freak has been jealous of me ever since we were kids, and now he's getting even. He's trying to ruin things for me, but I don't intend to let him get away with it."

Shocked, she gasped. "Lance, you don't know what you're saying!"

"I know exactly what I'm saying," he snarled. "I'm saying Neil can go to hell, and you can, too, for taking his side." And he turned and stomped out.

Nobody had ever talked to Cammy like that before. She supposed she had led a sheltered life, but her grandparents had been gentle, loving people. With her cousin's words echoing in her mind that night, she lay in bed for hours unable to sleep, wishing Lance would call and tell her he hadn't meant what he said. Finally she managed to doze off.

The ringing telephone woke her up the next morning, and she stumbled groggily out of bed and rushed out into the hall to answer it, stubbing her toe on the cedar chest at the foot of her bed as she went. "Hello?"

"Good morning, Cammy. This is Adam Neil."

"Oh…Adam." She felt like a punctured balloon. She'd hoped it was Lance, but he probably had no intention of apologizing.

"Don't act so happy to hear from me." Adam sounded dryly amused. "I'm not sure I can handle the flattery."

The thought of his one-sided smile made her spirits lift a little in spite of the miserable night she'd just spent. She could think of worse ways to start the day than with a telephone call from Adam Neil.

"I was just checking to see if you still want me to proceed with probating the will," he said. "You've talked to Lance by now, I guess?"

She rubbed a hand across her aching forehead. "Oh, yes!"

"Yes, you want me to go ahead, or yes, you've spoken to Lance?"

"Both. Did you think he would talk me into selling?"

"I figured he'd try."

"He did that, all right."

"But you stood your ground?"

Sighing, she slumped against the wall. "Mmm-hmm."

He was silent a minute, then asked, "Are you okay?"

The reluctant concern in his husky voice sent a liquid shiver through her veins. Cammy closed her eyes, savoring the feeling that Adam really seemed to care about her.

But it was clear that he didn't want to care. Anyway, she told herself, his interest was strictly that of an attorney for his client. There was nothing the least bit personal in it. He hadn't had a silly crush on *her* ever since he was fourteen years old, for goodness sake!

"I'm fine," she lied, adding politely, "As long as you handle the legal paperwork and tell me when to show up in court, you really don't have to concern yourself with my problems, Adam."

"Of course," he said, his voice suddenly devoid of all warmth. "I'll keep that in mind from now on."

She winced when she heard the gentle click of the connection being broken at the other end of the line. *Now you've done it, Cammy,* she thought dismally. *Is there anyone else you'd care to drive away while you're at it?*

Chapter Three

Cammy studied her reflection in the wall-sized mirror in the foyer of the Continental Café, searching for shadows under her eyes and other telltale signs of her recent sleep loss. She'd been practicing with some makeup lately—nothing heavy; just a touch of this and that. All things considered, she supposed she looked okay.

She'd worn her cheeriest outfit—a hot-pink cotton skirt and matching pink and turquoise T-shirt—and had even had her shoulder-length brown hair trimmed and curled into her usual pageboy style at a local beauty parlor earlier, because she wanted to give the impression that Cammy Anderson wasn't trudging around in the throes of depression.

Not that she would fool anyone, she figured morosely. Everybody probably already knew about her falling out with her cousins. That was what came from living in a town the size of Comanche.

She groaned, telling herself she should never have agreed to meet Margo here. Maybe she could sneak out before anyone saw her and hurry on back to the farm....

"There you are, Cammy!" Margo Reese blew in the door just then like a five-feet-tall, gale-force wind and grabbed her arm. She whisked Cammy into the restaurant, talking nonstop as she went. "Sorry I'm late, but I couldn't take my lunch break until somebody got back to the courthouse to cover for me. It's absolutely vital that the motor-vehicle department be open at all times, you know. It's just impossible to predict when an emergency will arise...a tractor needing new license plates, or some such earth-shattering dilemma that couldn't wait until one o'clock."

Giving up all hope of escaping, Cammy followed the wisecracking Margo to a rear corner booth, a smile plastered across her face and a wave for those diners that she knew.

Evidently her performance wasn't very convincing, though, because she hadn't taken more than two bites of her cheeseburger before her best friend tackled the problem head-on. "Okay, Camelia, what's bugging you? Why have you been hiding out at home for a week? And why were you about to run out on me when I got here?"

Cammy knew better than to play innocent. She jabbed a French fry into the catsup and then looked at it as if wondering what to do with it. Her long-lashed blue eyes lifted to meet Margo's. "I thought you would have heard by now. Everybody's furious at me."

Margo thumped her plump chest. "*I'm* not."

"Thank you." She managed a halfhearted smile. "Everyone else is, though."

"Oh, yeah? Who, for instance? You and Wesley broke up months ago, so you can't be mooning about that."

Cammy looked pained. "Margo, I'm not talking about Wesley Dean! I don't care if I never see that potential felon again." Long on passion and short on appeal, he'd tried once too often to get her into bed with him and had capped it off by declaring that he wanted to marry her, as if that would do the trick. She'd practically had to cry rape to make him understand she just wasn't interested. "It's not Wesley. It's . . . oh, it's everybody!"

Much as she hated to talk about her family, Cammy had been holding it inside for too long. She glanced around to be sure nobody could overhear, then told Margo what had been going on, concluding, "Now nobody will speak to me. I hoped I could smooth things over if I fixed a big Sunday dinner at the farm, but Babette and Joe Kenneth made excuses for not coming, and Lance wouldn't even get on the phone when I called. I asked Monica to pass along the invitation, but she said she didn't think it was a very good time for them."

Margo narrowed her eyes and her round, usually cherubic face reddened. "Why, those rotten sneaks! Hiring George Biggs to trick you into leaving your own home!" She gave Cammy a stern frown. "Surely you realize that it's no big loss if they never speak to you again. They'll just try to take advantage of you, as Adam Neil pointed out." Her expression underwent a swift change as a teasing humor lit her brown eyes. "At least you can take heart in the fact that Adam's on your side."

Cammy frowned. "Not anymore. I've alienated him, too."

"Oh, Cammy!" Margo clucked when she had heard the rest of the story. "No wonder you're so mad at yourself. I know how long you've been lusting after him."

"*Lusting* after him!" Cammy yelped, then darted a mortified look around to see if anybody had caught that.

With all the pink-cheeked dignity she could muster, she whispered, "I have never lusted after a man in my life."

Margo grinned. "Liar."

Disgruntled, she said, "Remind me never to confide in you again."

"Look, Cammy, join the twentieth century," Margo said unrepentantly. "So what if your hormones get a little stirred up whenever you see Adam? That's perfectly normal. Shoot, he makes *my* hormones go downright haywire! At least he calls you once in a while and stops by your house. And he lives right down the road from you. There's nothing but the Chappell place between his farm and yours."

"But Adam only calls or stops by on business."

"So? That's a start. If I could dream up some legal business for him to tend to, I would...just like April Magness. She may be rich, but she's not above scheming."

"What do you mean?"

"Oh, I saw her going into his office again this morning as I arrived at work. That's about the fifth time in two weeks." Margo waved a hand disdainfully. "I swear, that woman comes up with more excuses for consulting her attorney than an inmate on death row! But why not? April's husband is twice her age, and besides, Adam's the most interesting male in twenty-six counties. His scars don't matter."

Cammy silently agreed with Margo's assessment of Adam. His scars had been a part of him for such a long time and had faded almost to the point of being unnoticeable, so that she couldn't understand why they were the first thing most people mentioned about him.

Margo picked up her burger, then paused, her eyes twinkling. "Maybe I'll walk out without paying for my lunch today. Then when I get arrested, I can hire Adam to get me out of jail. Clever idea, huh?''

Reluctant laughter bubbled up from Cammy's throat, easing the ache deep inside her. Thank heavens for a crazy wonderful friend like Margo!

Something woke Cammy. She opened her eyes, disoriented, not knowing how long she'd been sleeping. It was pitch-black in her bedroom, so she figured it had to be the middle of the night. Her night-light seemed to have gone out, and the air-conditioning unit in the window was strangely silent. The electricity must be off for some reason.

In the summertime she always closed the door when she went to bed so the air conditioner could cool her room efficiently. Now the room was still and hot...unbearably hot. Her thin cotton nightgown was soaked with perspiration, her skin damp.

Sitting up and kicking back the sheet, Cammy grew suddenly conscious of the acrid sting of smoke in her nostrils. She took a deep breath, seeking fresh air, only to choke when she could find none. Dear Lord, she thought as she swung her legs over the edge of the bed, there was smoke everywhere!

''Fire!'' she muttered aloud, her eyes beginning to burn and tear. ''Stay calm! Dear God in heaven, keep me calm.''

At that moment a violent spasm of coughing almost doubled her over. Knowing that the safest air was supposed to be near the floor, she dropped down onto her hands and knees. All she could see through the dense smoke was a faint strip of orange glowing under the closed door. The fire must be out in the hallway.

Panic gripped her. How could she get out? Flames waited outside the door, and the only window was blocked by an air-conditioning unit that she couldn't hope to budge.

Cammy made the only choice she could. She hiked the tail of her nightgown up and tied it in a secure knot at her waist to keep it out of her way, then began crawling toward the doorway. Toward the fire.

The night was dark, with no moon in sight and only a handful of stars winking through the clouds. Adam stood on the edge of the circle driveway at the front of the house, his head thrown back to the sky as he inhaled the sweet scent of grass. Pete Blanco had come to mow the lawn today—all seven gently rolling acres of it—and the sprinklers had been watering the lush green St. Augustine until Adam had turned off the system just now.

A good rain would help, but he wasn't very hopeful. So far June had been dry and hot...a barren spell in more ways than one, Adam thought with restless discontent. But then he should be thoroughly accustomed to barren spells by now.

Sometimes he wished he had a perennially rosy outlook like Ted Nix, who leased Adam's farm and pastureland. Every time Adam saw him, Nix was expecting enough rain to provide grazing for his cattle. In addition, he anticipated sunny skies and bumper crops the rest of the time. And he usually got what he wanted; Ted had a way with the land, besides boasting a devoted wife and a handful of nice kids.

As for Adam himself, he didn't think he had it in him to hold such an optimistic attitude. Realism seemed to be too deeply ingrained in him.

He rolled his head from side to side and flexed his shoulders, feeling some of the tension from a too-long, too-busy day seep out of his muscles. Until ten minutes ago, he'd been seated for long neck-cramping hours at his desk inside, his shirtsleeves rolled back and his feet bare, catching up on paperwork that he'd brought home from the office. Then, when he'd glanced at the clock to see that it was after 2:00 a.m., Adam had called it quits and gone out to get some fresh air. It was just such country air, whipped across the fields by a brisk southerly breeze, that usually reassured him he'd made the right decision to move back here after he finished school. In spite of all that had happened here, this place near the heart of Texas was home to Adam, or as much a home as he would ever have.

Somewhere in the distance a dog was barking. He listened, wondering what had the animal so riled up, then filled his lungs once more before turning to go inside.

Suddenly Adam paused, exhaled in a sharp whoosh, and sniffed more cautiously. Was that smoke he smelled? He looked around but saw nothing out of the ordinary and almost decided it was his imagination. Then he turned his face toward the wind and got another strong whiff of it. There was no mistaking it—something was burning!

Cursing his bare feet, Adam hurried through the wet grass along the front of the house and turned the corner. From that point, because his home had been built atop a knoll, he had a panoramic view of a vast stretch of country to the south, and what he saw made him stop and gasp, his heart tumbling over. The old wood-framed Anderson house, less than a mile away down the paved county road, was engulfed in flames that were shooting high into the sky.

"Oh, God, no!" Adam whispered in a strangled plea, his body frozen. It was his worst nightmare come true, and the awful, immobilizing fear slammed through him with every pounding beat of his heart. The memory of flames clawed at his mind . . . angry flames licking at his face, his chest, his hands and arms and legs.... It was a memory that never entirely went away, and it was suddenly all around him.

For several endless seconds the terror paralyzed him, and then he had one clear thought: *Cammy!* Cammy Anderson was in that house. Somebody had to get her out.

Adam gave himself a ferocious mental shake, fighting down the sick feeling of dread that was making hash of his insides, and forced his body to move. Reaching into his pocket for the keys, he ran to his car, started the engine, and tore out of the driveway before he even remembered he was wearing no shoes. It didn't matter.

By the time he reached the burning house, he had called in a fire alarm on his car telephone.

By the time he parked and jumped out of the car at the edge of the yard, he knew who was going to have to go inside for Cammy. The firemen would never make it all the way out from town in time.

It was like willing himself to jump into a roaring furnace. It was without a doubt the worst moment of his life, or at least a close second. For an instant, standing beside his car, Adam wasn't sure he could make himself move forward again, but then an image of Cammy arose...a solemn, sweet-faced young thing who was so obviously innocent and naive and trusting that there should have been a law against her being so damned alone. He couldn't let her die.

Please, God, don't let it be too late! Focusing grimly on that prayer, he ran up onto the porch, kicked in the door, and plunged headfirst into the inferno.

Later Adam couldn't say how he did it. His familiarity with the farmhouse, dating back to childhood visits in the company of his mother, explained how he knew to head straight down the hall, which was where he found Cammy when he almost tripped over her. But nobody understood how he scooped her up out of the smoke and flames and made it back outside with neither of them receiving anything but a few superficial blisters.

Once they were free of the house, Adam kept going blindly. He carried Cammy the hundred yards to the barn before his legs buckled and he sank down onto a pile of hay, still cradling her in his arms. They both sat coughing and gulping in air until their lungs seemed clear of smoke, and then they lay back exhausted on the straw.

Adam was slick with sweat and on the verge of losing his usual rational control, but he was still coherent enough to note that Cammy was shaking even worse than he was. Trying to hold back her sobs and failing miserably, she whimpered softly, "Dear God, I was so scared! I thought I was going to die, Adam!"

Almost too tired to move, he slowly lifted his head to study her. A rush of tender concern pulsed through him at the bedraggled yet somehow appealing picture she made, her huge eyes glittering with tears that coursed in pale rivulets down her smoke-blackened cheeks, her hair spread out tousled and wild-looking on his chest.

The tenderness took Adam by surprise, and at first he refused to acknowledge it. He didn't want to be feeling that way, especially after what Cammy had said to him last week. "Keep your nose out of my personal life," or something to that effect. He'd told himself several times since then that that was fine with him; Adam Neil had no particular interest in *anybody's* personal life. If it hadn't been for his overdeveloped sense of justice and a promise he'd made to an old lady, he never would have been having that conversation with Cammy in the first place....

Suddenly his drifting gaze reached her nightgown, and he swallowed his supposed indifference with a gulp. The white cotton garment was all torn and grimy and tangled around her hips, exposing the pale soft curve of her breasts at the neckline and leaving her slim legs bare. She huddled against him, crying as quietly as she could, and a hard fierce knot formed in his gut. The tenderness, it seemed, was rapidly turning to gnawing hunger, and hunger under these circumstances was ridiculous.

"It's okay, Cammy," he murmured hoarsely. "You'll be okay."

"Will I?" She sounded desperate for reassurance. Her heart was trying to pound its way out of her chest, and a storm of emotion had her totally confused as to just what was going on inside her—distress over her burning house, or gripping, electric awareness of the man whose arms held her?

He closed his eyes and used one hand to draw her face into the angle of his neck and shoulder. "I promise, Cammy, you will."

"And you, Adam?" she whispered uncertainly. "Will you be okay?"

Before he could answer her, the fire trucks arrived, followed by an ambulance, and Adam had to pry his hands from Cammy so she could be examined and given some oxygen. The ambulance crew expressed concern for Adam, too, but neither would consent to being taken to the hospital.

"It's nothing short of a miracle," the paramedic said when he finished, shaking his head in wonder, "but you're both okay. Except for those blisters," he said, gesturing at Adam's bandaged feet. "Care to tell me how you made it through the flames without shoes, Mr. Neil?"

He gave a tense shrug. "I can't."

Cammy sat on the stretcher that had been removed from the ambulance, her back to the firemen who were still dousing water on the smoking remains. Unable to bear watching, or to think about what was going to happen now that her home was gone, she focused her thoughts on the man sitting on another stretcher nearby. She wasn't sure what to think about Adam...not after the feelings he'd evoked when he held her. It was like seeing him for the very first time, and yet it was like uncovering an ageless truth that she'd always suspected about him: He could make her *feel* as nobody else ever had!

Sighing, she pushed back her tangled hair from her cheek. The only thing she knew for sure was that Adam had saved her life tonight, and she couldn't begin to imagine what it had cost him. Like her, he kept his face averted from the fire, and he still appeared dazed, his eyes shadowed with some inner, secret hurt too terrible to share.

Not that she imagined Adam ever shared his pain with others. For the past half hour Cammy had been observing the way he was trying to gather up the threads of his tattered composure, to rebuild the wall of reserve that usually enclosed him securely. That he had to try so hard was proof that tonight had just about been the limit for him.

At some point he realized his sleeves were rolled up, and he immediately pulled them down and buttoned the cuffs. *Scars,* she thought and felt a distinct tugging at her heart.

Cammy stood on shaky legs and walked over to him. "Thank you, Adam." Raw emotion sent a tremor through her words.

He looked up at her quickly, knowing without asking what she was thanking him for. At the sight of her standing with clasped hands right in front of him, an involuntary smile lifted one corner of his lips. One of the paramedics had wrapped her in his white coat, and it hung loosely on her. Smudges of soot still streaked her heart-shaped face. And in spite of all that, Adam briefly entertained the notion of sweeping her up against him and kissing the tears from her lashes.

Lord, he must be going crazy! His mouth straightened into a stern line. "For heaven's sake, Cammy, sit down before you fall down."

And while those cool words still echoed in her ears, she heard Lance exclaim from halfway across the yard, "Cammy, you look like hell! Thank the Lord you're okay."

Lance! Cammy's hopes soared as she whirled around. Maybe he was ready to forgive her. Beside her, Adam turned to watch as her cousin approached them.

"Mr. Chappell telephoned and told me about the fire, and I came right out," Lance said. He glanced at the blackened ruins behind Cammy and whistled. "What a mess!"

Taken aback by his jaunty attitude, Cammy could only stare at him. This home that he was dismissing so casually had been built by their grandparents; their fathers, who were brothers, had grown up in it. Cammy herself had lived here all her life. Every memento she cherished had just burned to ashes.

Lance didn't seem to notice her shocked expression. "I guess there's no question now that you'll sell."

"Sell?" she echoed, not believing what she was hearing.

"Of course. What would be the point in keeping it? There's no longer any place here for you to live." Rather belatedly he added, "I'm sorry it's gone, Cammy. But maybe it's for the best."

Suddenly Adam was on his gauze-wrapped feet, standing toe-to-toe with Lance. Cammy had never seen anything like the fury flashing in Adam's eyes just then. "Shut up!" he said in a low, deadly voice. "If you say one more word tonight about selling this place, I'll break your nose."

Lance jumped backward. "I have every right—"

"I don't give a damn for your rights. Cammy has stood just about all she can, and I'm not going to let you make it any worse. Why don't you go on back where you came from? You can talk to her some other time."

"You bet your life I will!" Lance fumed, then looked at her resentfully. "Where am I supposed to find you?"

"She's staying at my house," Adam said before Cammy could open her mouth.

Although Lance's scowl indicated his disapproval of such an arrangement, he apparently deduced from Adam's blunt tone that it was pointless to protest. Cammy understood that, too. She was staying with Adam. End of discussion.

The funny thing was, it didn't even occur to her to argue. In fact, Adam's announcement sent a wave of warm, bewildering excitement zinging through her.

Chapter Four

Flame-colored ribbons of dawn had begun to etch the sky by the time Adam finished conferring with the fire chief and sheriff and started toward home with Cammy. Too mentally exhausted for words, she could only sit numbly beside him as he drove the short distance and parked on the paved circular driveway in front of the graceful, spacious, pink brick house that had been built by his parents.

Just as he got out of the car and came around to help Cammy, the housekeeper opened the front door. "Here we are," Adam said gruffly.

She looked at the house, suddenly uncertain she should have come here. Even in the dim light before day had taken hold, the white shutters trimming the windows and the columns along the front verandah had a pristine quality that made Cammy feel out of place. "I'm so dirty," she began.

He managed a one-sided grin. "That's certainly not a permanent condition. Tally will have you bathed and in bed before you know it." When she still hesitated, he added dryly, "I promise you, it won't hurt a bit."

That ended Cammy's protests. Inside, she discovered that, sure enough, Talese Blackraven already had a bath waiting and the blue-sprigged sheet and matching comforter turned back on the bed in the adjoining guest bedroom. How she had known to expect company, Cammy couldn't imagine, although rumors abounded that the full-blooded Comanche Indian possessed all sorts of mysterious talents.

Of indeterminate age and marital status, the close-mouthed Talese had been with Adam's family since his early childhood. She was built along the lines of a stately Amazon—as tall as her dark master and thirty pounds heavier, her movements slow and determined. Her black hair was pinned back in a stern-looking knot on her neck. Few would have dared to argue when she said, as she did to Cammy, "Give me your clothes, missy, and get in the tub."

Cammy found herself obeying wordlessly under the unwavering gaze of Talese Blackraven, stripping off the paramedic's white coat and her own ruined nightgown, then slipping gratefully into the steaming bathwater and accepting the thick washcloth and new bar of soap from the older woman. Silently Talese left the bathroom, only to return when Cammy had finished soaking, lathering, and rinsing, to hand her a huge fluffy towel. Wrapping herself in the bath sheet, Cammy thought she'd never felt anything so luxurious in her entire life.

Minutes later she slid beneath the bedclothes, wearing the white T-shirt Talese had given her—Adam's shirt, she was certain. Although freshly laundered, it smelled like him, and that caused a pleasant disturbance in her pulse rate. Adoring the soft feel of the cotton against her skin, she settled down to rest in cool, clean comfort.

At that point she was forced to amend her earlier opinion: The bath sheet had been nice, but *this* was the most sumptuous, the most lavishly agreeable experience imaginable. It was sheer heaven. If only she could manage not to think about why she was here....

As if she'd foreseen what nightmares lay in store for Cammy, just then the woman brought in a cup of some strange, strong-smelling tea. "Drink this," she said in her rather gravelly voice. "It will help you sleep."

Cammy sat up in bed. "What is it, decaf?"

"Made from herbs," Talese responded, unsmiling, then waited for Cammy to return the cup, which she did as soon as she could swallow all the hot, bitter liquid.

Too late, Cammy wondered what kind of herbs Talese might have put in the tea, but within minutes after she had nestled back into the downy-soft covers, she felt too relaxed to worry about potentially poisonous herbs or burning houses or anything else.

She slept soundly, and when she awoke, there was no soreness or lingering muscle tension to remind her of last night's horror. There was only the delicious sense of being cosseted and pampered in some beautiful room of ivory lace curtains and blue-patterned wallpaper, with warmly polished oak furniture and a thick blue carpet on the floor. A room fit for a princess, Cammy thought, in one of the loveliest homes in the county—Adam Neil's.

But even as she lay stretching in the bed, the awareness of why Adam had brought her here to spend the night came back to settle heavily and painfully on her chest. Gran and Grandpa's house had burned down. Cammy had no place to go and not a stitch of clothes to put on. Everything she owned, except for the land itself and a car that had seen better days, had been destroyed. Her old life as she knew it had just ended, and she was going to have to forge a new life for herself. Doing what, she didn't know.

She exhaled aloud, at the same moment that Talese cracked the door to look in from the hallway. Seeing Cammy awake, the woman opened the door wider and brought in an armload of clothes still in plastic bags from the local department store. As she deposited some of the bags on a chair and hung the others in the closet, she said, "These are for you."

Cammy sat up hurriedly. "Where did they come from? I'm afraid I can't afford—"

"Adam can afford," Talese interrupted. "If they do not please you, he will exchange them." She nodded at the chair on her way to the door. "All you will need is there. Adam waits to see you. You should eat now anyway." And she left before Cammy could digest all her imperiously delivered information.

"Aye, aye, Cap'n." She saluted the closed door.

She had no idea what time it was, but judging from the waning daylight visible through the window, she had slept much of the day. Chagrined, Cammy got up and inspected the purchases Adam had sent via Talese. She discovered, as the housekeeper promised, all the essentials she could possibly need, from hairbrush and deodorant to a generous supply of silky lingerie in a rainbow of delicate colors.

Moving quickly to the closet, she selected a simple sage-colored dress with a drop-waist, cap sleeves, and a matching cardigan jacket made from the same soft cotton knit. The price tags on all the items had already been removed, which simplified the task of dressing, but Cammy made a mental note to ask Talese for the receipts so she could repay Adam...perhaps by taking out a bank loan, she thought worriedly.

As she smoothed the sheer nylons up over her slim legs and slid her feet into remarkably comfortable leather pumps, Cammy couldn't help marveling that Adam had guessed her clothing sizes with such accuracy. One would think he shopped for young ladies every day.

Maybe he did, she thought. After all, did anybody in Comanche really know what Adam did in his spare time? He was always going out of town on "business." He might have a dozen girlfriends in Dallas or even New York. The idea disturbed her more than it should have and set her to speculating exactly what kind of woman would appeal to Adam. One blessed with beauty, money, and a good education, no doubt....

"Three strikes and I'm out," she muttered. In spite of that, and even though she realized she was keeping Adam waiting, Cammy took great pains with her hair and face. The makeup kit and styling mousse that she found in one bag certainly helped, but that didn't entirely calm the butterflies in her stomach as she went in search of her host.

The sound of voices guided her into the large, formal living room, which was graciously appointed in traditional cream-upholstered furniture. Cammy's prepared speech of thanks flew right out of her head when she found Adam talking to Lance.

Actually Lance seemed to be doing most of the talking, but as soon as he caught sight of her, he broke off to stand and give her a disgruntled look. "I was beginning to think you were never going to get up, Cammy. I've been here nearly an hour."

"Sorry." She started to excuse herself by saying she didn't know he was waiting—only that Adam was—but she didn't want to cause trouble for the housekeeper.

Adam had stood, too, upon her entrance, and the expression on his face led her to wonder what words had passed between the two men before she arrived on the scene. "Cammy had a rough night," he said in a voice that sounded tight, controlled. "She needed to rest."

"Of course," Lance agreed hastily. With a show of concern, he gestured to the sofa behind him. "Come on, Cammy, sit down. I think we'd better talk."

She sat beside her cousin, and Adam resumed his seat nearby. Although Lance clearly would have preferred him to leave the room, it was just as clear that to suggest such a thing was out of the question.

Before anyone broke the silence, Talese Blackraven appeared in the double doorway leading to the dining room and beyond that, to the kitchen. Adam looked over at her. "Yes, Tally?"

"Supper is ready for the young miss."

"Fine. Bring it in here, please."

As Talese turned to obey, Adam stood again and retrieved a small folding table from the dining room, which he set up in front of Cammy. When he crossed the room, she realized he was limping very slightly. The blisters!

The reminder of how he had saved her life made her heart hurt, and she swallowed past the lump in her throat to ask, "How are your feet?"

"Fine," he said.

Cammy doubted that. She figured the shoes, polished wing tips that looked stiff and uncomfortable, weren't helping the situation much, but she bit back the suggestion that he take them off. Adam Neil, in his usual garb of business suit and tie, was not likely to take off his shoes and go barefoot while he had company—not even if his shoes rubbed the blisters raw and made them bleed.

Talese served Cammy then, which forced Lance to wait rather impatiently while she ate as much as she could of the liberal portions of stew and salad made from garden vegetables. The meal was hearty and filling, and Cammy thanked the woman sincerely when she removed the tray.

The moment Cammy's plate was taken away, Lance got right down to business. "Okay, Cammy, let's talk about what you're going to do now."

She caught her lower lip between her teeth and bit down hard for a second, then released it and sighed. "I don't know. I've been wondering that myself."

Lance rapped a drumbeat along his jaw with his fingertips, trying to look thoughtful. "The way I see it, you're in quite a dilemma. No place to live, no way to earn a living. Looks to me like you'd better do what I've been suggesting all along."

"Sell the farm, you mean?" she asked huskily, her blue eyes clouded.

He nodded. "You can pay for one of those training courses we talked about before. That's your best shot at getting a decent job. Until we sell the place, I suppose you'll have to come stay with us. I talked Monica into agreeing that you could sleep on the couch for a couple of weeks."

Cammy felt a stab of pain at Lance's words. He made it sound as if her presence would be a major imposition, as she supposed it would, in his already crowded household.

"Thank you for the invitation," she said. "It's kind of you and Monica to have me." Out of the corner of her eye, she saw Adam cross and then uncross his long legs, but she didn't turn to look at him.

"That's okay," Lance said magnanimously. "It's no problem, as long as we get things moving on the sale again.

If we're lucky, Mr. Crenshaw might agree to advance you some money even before everything's finalized, so you can get yourself an apartment and enroll in some kind of school.''

"Tell me, Anderson, just what kind of school did you have in mind for Cammy?" Adam spoke up quietly.

Lance shrugged. "Whatever career she decides on. Beauty operator, nurse, secretary. She can take one of those truck-driving courses if she wants to. It's Cammy's life."

"You're right about that," Adam said, getting to his feet. He paced a few steps and then, his mouth bracketed with sudden deep lines, sat back down in his chair to face Cammy directly. "Do you want to go to school?"

Cammy felt all the usual fluttery sensations prickle along her nerves when Adam looked at her, the same old breathlessness he always seemed to arouse in her, but she tried to ignore the feelings. It was her future they were talking about here, and it looked much too dim for her to be letting her attention wander off on some romantic tangent. "It doesn't seem to matter what I want to do, Adam. At the moment I don't have much choice but to go to school or get a job. And I seriously doubt if anyone would hire me."

"That's right. She's really got no choice at all," Lance said, his voice so smug that Adam rounded on him with a look that should have sliced him to the bone.

"And why is that?" Adam's tone was steel-edged, and his gray eyes glinted dangerously. "She had a few more options until her house burned down, didn't she?" When Lance merely looked uncomfortable, Adam said, "Are you aware, Anderson, that the fire chief suspects some-one may have deliberately set the blaze? Rather convenient for you that her last claim to independence was destroyed by the fire, wasn't it?''

Lance's face went pale. ''Exactly what are you suggesting?''

''At the moment, nothing. But you can forget it if you plan to benefit from Cammy's misfortune.'' Adam turned to her. ''There's no need for you to move. I have plenty of room, so you won't have to sleep on the sofa. You're welcome here, not an intruder as your cousin would make you feel at his house. Nor do you have to sell your farm. That wasn't what your grandmother wanted for you.''

Cammy gazed at Adam in speechless amazement, while Lance jumped up to protest. ''Wait a minute! This is crazy, Cammy. You can't stay here! What would people think? Maybe... maybe it won't be necessary for you to sleep on our sofa, after all. The kids could probably double up so you can use one of their bedrooms—''

But Adam went on as if Lance hadn't spoken. ''Perhaps it's time you knew, Cammy, that before she died, your grandmother told me her greatest concern was for you, for what would happen to you after she was gone. I promised her then that I would do whatever was necessary to see that your future was secure. And I don't take my promises lightly.''

He flicked a hard look at Lance, then concentrated on her again, the intensity of his stare making Cammy's pulse jerk. How on earth did he plan to fulfill his vow to Gran? Several wild possibilities shot through her mind, but nothing prepared her for Adam's next words. He looked her straight in the eye and said, ''I intend to take care of you, and it occurs to me that the best way to do that is to marry you.''

Marry her? He wanted to *marry* her? Cammy sank back, shaken, her wide eyes never leaving Adam's face.

Was he joking? Was this some scheme he'd concocted to outbluff Lance, to try to keep her cousins from pushing her around?

Lance appeared ready to have an apoplectic fit. Red-faced, he stalked toward Adam and halted, his fists clenched at his sides. "You have the nerve to talk about marrying Cammy?" He whirled to glare at her. "If someone really did burn down the house, you'd do well to suspect *him*. He was the first person on the scene, and I guess everybody knows about his experience in starting fires!"

"Lance!" Cammy objected, glancing quickly at Adam and finding him tight-lipped, the expression on his face inscrutable, as though carved in stone.

"Well, it's true," Lance went on. "His brother would be alive today if Adam hadn't been so handy with gasoline and a box of matches."

Cammy shut her eyes and shook her head in mute protest to what Lance was saying. But he wasn't finished.

"Open your eyes and look at him, Cammy. Take a good look."

Almost as if she couldn't help herself, she did, and Adam's shuttered eyes met hers, still not giving away what he was thinking or feeling behind that rigid mask.

"Could you stand to live with him? Someone capable of killing his own brother? Do you want to see those scars every day of your life? Wouldn't it bother you to have everybody in town think you're so desperate for a man that you'd marry one as unsociable...as downright ugly as Adam Neil?"

Ugly? Adam? Cammy had to fight to control the hysterical smile that tugged at her lips. If Lance only knew how often she'd daydreamed about marrying Adam Neil! Gran's teasing hadn't helped much, either. Yes, Adam was scarred, but he was far from ugly, as any female in

Comanche between the ages of ten and ninety could testify. Only men like Lance seemed not to recognize that fact.

As for Adam's having the capacity to hurt his brother... well, the idea was too preposterous to warrant a response. Cammy knew deep in her heart that he would never have set fire to her house or anyone else's.

She gave a distracted head shake and turned back to her cousin. "You're forgetting that Adam saved my life last night."

Lance snorted. "Don't tell me you'd marry him out of gratitude for his heroism!" He made a frustrated gesture with one hand. "You might just as well marry him out of pity. But I'm warning you, Cammy, if you do, you'll probably live to regret it. In fact, I guarantee you'll regret it the rest of your life."

Frowning absently, Cammy had to agree. She was thinking that if she *did* marry Adam, it certainly wouldn't be out of gratitude or pity, both of which she considered to be poor reasons to spend the rest of her life with anyone.

"You know," Lance said, calming down again when Cammy didn't reject his argument, "since your attorney brought up the subject, it might not be such a bad idea for you to get married. I can name at least one eligible bachelor who would jump at the chance of marrying you—one who rates my wholehearted stamp of approval, too. He'd be a perfect mate for you."

Cammy's head was beginning to ache from the tension that she could feel vibrating between the men, and she suddenly seemed to be having trouble following Lance's meaning. She gave him a puzzled look, and he said, "Wesley Dean." When she still seemed blank, he added, "You used to date Wesley, remember?"

Lord, did she ever! If Wesley was Lance's idea of a perfect mate for her, she'd better be thankful marriages were no longer arranged by families.

"So how about it?" Lance pursued the subject.

She leaned back against the cushions, eyeing her cousin wearily. "I can't think of anything I'd like to do less than marry Wesley Dean."

"I wouldn't be so quick to dismiss him if I were you," Lance said. "He's respected around here—"

"In case you didn't understand her, Camelia isn't interested in marrying Dean," Adam cut in coldly, getting to his feet. "Now if you're finished, my housekeeper will show you out."

Cammy stood, too, and unconsciously began massaging her throbbing temples with one hand. "I think it probably would be best if you left now, Lance. I don't feel like talking."

Lance opened his mouth to protest, but at that moment Talese Blackraven appeared as if by magic. Adam took Cammy's arm and led her from the room, leaving her cousin little choice but to make his departure under Talese's stern eye.

Expecting to be allowed to return to her bedroom, Cammy was surprised when Adam escorted her down the hall into a bookcase-lined room that must be his study. He shut the door behind them and motioned her to a seat on a comfortable blue corduroy-upholstered sofa, then came to stand right in front of her, crossing his arms on his chest.

"Well, Cammy?" he asked.

She tipped her head back and looked up at him. Usually she *liked* to look at him, but the grimly stubborn set to his chin and the determination glinting in his eyes worried her. Too much had happened in the past twenty-four hours—in the two months since Gran died, really—and she wasn't sure she could cope just now with whatever was on Adam's mind.

"I'm tired," she said. "Can this possibly wait until tomorrow?"

"No, it can't," he denied flatly. And then, in the least romantic tone imaginable, he said, "How about it, Cammy? Will you marry me?"

Chapter Five

There it was again—the last thing in the world that
Cammy would ever have expected to hear from Adam
Neil: A marriage proposal. She studied his face suspiciously for some sign of amusement. She could see none,
but then she figured he was very good at hiding his emotions. Just to be on the safe side, she asked, "Are you
joking?"

A small line formed between his dark eyebrows. "Does
this strike you as a subject I would joke about?"

"No..." Honesty compelled her to add, "It doesn't
strike me as a subject that you'd discuss with me at all."

"Or with anyone else?" he prompted, his chilly tone
indicating sudden withdrawal.

"I don't have a clue what you might talk about with
other people, Adam." She shook her head in bewilder-
ment. "You're my lawyer, and you've been one of my
nearest neighbors as far back as I can remember, but we've
never been what you would call close friends. Besides,

you're so much older...." She stopped, blushing at her lack of tact. She was going about this all wrong, but then that seemed to be typical behavior for her whenever Adam was around. He always shook her up so she couldn't think straight! Clearing her throat, she tried again. "Not that you're exactly *old* or anything, but you've never...I mean...we've never even been out on a date."

As she rambled on, his cool expression began to show signs of defrosting. She could have sworn she actually saw his lips twitch, but when he answered, his words were crisp. "Nevertheless, Cammy, I can assure you I've never been more serious." He uncrossed his arms and moved to sit behind his desk. That seemed to lend credibility to his words—as if he were discussing a legal matter with her instead of pursuing the unbelievable topic of their potential matrimony. "As I told you earlier, I promised your grandmother before she died that I would look after you, and it's becoming more apparent with every passing day that you need me."

Cammy wasn't sure how she felt about that. Her doubts must have shown in her wide blue eyes, because he dragged his fingers through his hair impatiently, leaving it attractively ruffled. "I thought by now you understood that your cousins have their own best interests at heart when it comes to the disposition of your grandmother's will, and that doesn't necessarily coincide with what's best for you. You *did* ask me to take charge, since you don't have the legal expertise?" Pausing, he lifted both eyebrows and waited for her assent.

Reluctantly she nodded. It still pained her soul to admit it, but Lance and his sister and brother had definitely pitted themselves squarely against her.

"I'm glad we're in agreement about that," he said with a trace of dryness. For a moment he hesitated, appearing to search for the right words, but finally he met her gaze straight on. "We have to consider the possibility that someone set fire to the house while you were sleeping, Cammy," he said quietly. "If that's the case, your life could be in danger." Before she could protest, he held up a hand. "I know you think nobody would try to hurt you, and I hope you're right. But that's a chance I'm not prepared to take. Not when it's so easy for me to keep you safe."

"By marrying me, you mean?" she said faintly.

"That's right. By marrying you. It's the ideal solution."

"Ideal?" she echoed in amazement. She reminded herself that he couldn't be acting out of fondness for her since, as she'd pointed out, he had never so much as asked her for a date in all the years they'd known each other. "Tell me, Adam, in what way would marriage be the ideal solution?"

"To put it simply, I can provide what you need—a home, legal advice, financial security while you get your life in order and decide what you want to do. I won't pressure you into making a hasty decision, possibly the *wrong* decision, as your cousins no doubt will try to do if they get the chance. You'll be able to concentrate all your energy and attention on preparing for the future, rather than merely struggling to survive from day to day."

She had to give him credit for making his suggestion sound sensible. In fact, she almost caught herself nodding agreement to his proposal. Hastily she said, "But marriage, Adam! It's so...so drastic!"

"Yes, but it's also quite respectable. If I were to offer you my hospitality and assistance without benefit of my name, people would be scandalized. On the other hand, if you marry me, you'll have all the time, money, and freedom you could wish for while you settle on a career, and nobody will dare to criticize you." From the hard note that edged his voice, she began to suspect Lance's earlier snide remarks about what people would say must have gotten to Adam more than he let on.

Cammy sighed, thinking that she would never understand what made Adam Neil tick. Here was a handsome, utterly fascinating man that probably half the women in the county secretly fantasized about, and he seemed bent on persuading plain, unremarkable Camelia Anderson to marry him! Didn't he know he could probably marry anyone he wanted?

She wished suddenly that she could talk things over with someone who had a level head, someone whose judgment she trusted. Better yet, she wished that for just half an hour, her best friend could be a fly on the wall and listen in on this absurd discussion. Margo would get a real kick out of it, although she would no doubt declare that Cammy had lost her ever-loving mind not to grab Adam while she had the chance.

Cammy was beginning to think maybe she *had* lost her mind, because as much as the idea of marrying Adam enticed her, she knew very well she couldn't say yes. A hundred and one objections kept popping up, the most persistent one being her certainty that Adam didn't care at all for her... not romantically, at any rate, which was the only way that counted here. What would happen when he grew tired of being saddled with her welfare and wanted to marry someone else—someone prettier and more sophisticated?

She wished she dared to just come right out and ask point-blank if he had a girlfriend somewhere who might not be keen on sharing him. Instead she said tentatively, "But marriage is such a permanent solution...."

"Do you have any idea how high the national divorce rate is? Marriage doesn't have to be permanent," he said, which wasn't exactly the reassurance she had been hoping to hear. "Once you've determined what you want to do with your future and are equipped to make it on your own, we can end the marriage if you wish." Misinterpreting her expression he added, "It will be a quiet divorce, I assure you. I'll see that you come out of it well-fixed." The right side of his mouth curved up into a smile so twisted yet somehow attractive that it pulled relentlessly at Cammy's heart. "If you leave me, you won't have to worry about mudslinging or nasty recriminations. I'll be the most discreet and amicable ex-husband you could ask for."

Cammy mulled that over. His proposal was sounding more and more implausibly generous...unless he already knew that he was eventually going to want a divorce.

Abruptly she stood up and moved around the room, trailing one hand over a leather-bound book that lay on a lamp table, then glancing distractedly at a small framed oil painting next to the door. Finally she returned to her seat and gave him a serious frown. "Adam, I can't let you do all this for me. You don't owe me anything. In fact, I owe *you*. You saved my life."

"Forget about that," he said curtly, leaving no room for doubt that he meant it. He didn't want her gratitude. "Believe me, what I'm proposing won't cost enough for me to notice. I can afford to support you, Cammy."

A tinge of pink stained her cheeks. "I'm sure you can, Adam, but..."

When she paused, he cut in so gruffly that she knew he'd drawn the wrong conclusions from her discomfiture. "If you're worrying about being a 'kept' woman, you can stop. I won't make any offensive demands or unwanted advances. You'll be safe here. I won't ask you to sleep with me."

Even as she felt her face turning from pink to red, she recognized that she felt more disappointed than relieved at his reassurance. "That's not what I was worrying about," she managed to say, her fingers locked together on her lap.

"Then what is it that's bothering you?" he demanded bluntly.

It took her several long seconds to formulate her answer, and even then she didn't sound very certain. "I guess... I just can't help wondering *why*. Why you would want to do this. Why you'd go to such lengths to help me."

"What's in it for me, you mean?"

"No!" She shook her head vigorously. "I don't think there's anything in it for you. Mostly I just wonder if you've really thought this over." She took a deep breath and blurted out the real issue. "That's what bothers me. That you should give up the chance for a truly happy marriage... give up your privacy... give up so much for nothing. Why, Adam?"

Why, indeed? Adam found it ironically amusing that his young client—the same trembling waif that he'd snatched, half-naked and scared out of her wits, from the flames of death the night before—that Cammy Anderson was sitting here now counseling him gravely on the wisdom of what he was trying to do. That she was trying to protect him from his own rashness.

The truth was, Adam had given plenty of thought to his proposal. He'd thought of little else ever since the idea first came to him after he'd brought Cammy home this morning. Although he'd cleaned up and then gone on to his law firm in town, intending to do some work, he had instead spent the entire day in a virtual haze, staring blankly out his office window as he examined this idea from every conceivable angle. After listing every pro and con he could think of, he was convinced it was the best way to go. Furthermore, he was grimly determined to persuade Cammy to say yes. He wasn't going to let her greedy cousins manipulate her into selling the family farm. No matter what, he refused to let them take advantage any more than they already had.

That there might be another, more subtly tempting reason behind his single-minded determination to marry Cammy, Adam wouldn't even let himself consider. He intended to protect her. That was all. There was no such thing as a "truly happy marriage," as Cammy had put it—at least not in his future. Romance had no place in his world.

"I've thought this over," he said in a low, firm voice. "Despite what you think, marrying you won't significantly alter my life or impede my happiness." His mouth quirked at that, but he didn't elaborate on his jaded opinion about happiness, knowing Cammy already considered him a hopeless cynic. He forced himself to continue evenly. "I've never found anyone else that I'd care to marry, and for the record, I'm not interested in bringing children into a world like this one. So you see, you won't be denying me any of those pleasures if you agree to marry me."

He was making an effort not to sound bitter, and that created an enormous lump in Cammy's throat, because it enabled her to see clearly how bitter he *was*. Bitter and lonely, she thought, studying him with soft, troubled eyes.

Just then he raised one hand and rubbed his left cheek in a preoccupied gesture that convinced her his bitterness and loneliness were rooted in his scars, if not even further back. Back to his childhood, probably. Which perhaps said something about his grim condemnation of her family.

If only she knew him better! If only she knew what had made him the way he was, she might be able to help.

A warm, unbidden tenderness for Adam enveloped Cammy at that thought, almost causing her to gasp aloud from the sheer force of it, and she wanted suddenly, more than she'd ever wanted anything, to fight the demons that tormented him. She ached to overcome his terrible bitterness, to fill up his life with laughter and love so he had no room for loneliness.

Will you listen to yourself, Cammy! she thought, getting a grip on her emotions before they could run away with her. Those were fine, lofty ambitions, but what made her think she could accomplish them? It wasn't as though Adam really cared about her. It wasn't as if he were asking for her help.

She exhaled quietly, wistfully, and looked over to see Adam watching her. The intensity of the expression in his smoky eyes unnerved her, and she got quickly to her feet. If she stayed here much longer, she would end up agreeing to do anything he asked of her and to heck with the consequences. "I'm really tired, Adam. If it's all right with you, I'd like to go to bed now."

Frustrated, he stood too. "You haven't given me an answer."

"I need some time to think about . . . about your offer." But she didn't really believe that more time would bring a solution. Her head was already spinning from thinking about Adam's strange marriage proposal. She wanted to please him almost as much as she yearned to help him, but she wasn't completely crazy. Even if his idea solved some of her problems, at the same time it would create new ones.

"We'll talk tomorrow, then." He sounded calm enough.

As she said good-night and left his study, she noticed his hand move to his face again, the fingertips tracing over the uneven blemishes that they obviously knew far too well already.

That image haunted her through her shower. Once in bed, she began to puzzle over why Adam seemed to care so much whether or not she married him. She wished she could believe that he harbored a hitherto secret passion for her, but she knew better. He'd come right out and told her not to expect anything physical from their union. It must be, as he said, that he felt a sense of duty and strong neighborly concern for her. After all, he had given his word to her grandmother that he would look after her.

Well, if he didn't want her gratitude, *she* didn't want him to feel obliged to do anything on her behalf. What kind of marriage would that be? Sooner or later he would start resenting her, or worse.

Cammy was just working herself up into a righteous dither when the housekeeper tapped on the door and asked if she needed anything. She didn't, but thanked Talese for her thoughtfulness.

"Adam was worried," the woman said flatly, letting Cammy know it hadn't been her concern but her boss's that prompted the inquiry.

Guessing that Talese probably resented her presence in the house, Cammy sat up and switched on the lamp beside the bed. "Miss Blackraven, I'm sorry if my being here is causing you extra work. I don't think I'll be staying long, but while I am here, you just tell me what I can do to help. I'm used to earning my keep."

Talese had been about to go, but she turned back at Cammy's words. "Why do you not stay?" she demanded, her eyes sharp, almost angry looking.

"Well, I . . ." Cammy couldn't help stammering under the glare she was receiving from the woman. She had thought Talese would be glad to hear she wasn't staying.

"I feel uncomfortable here. All these clothes he bought— I can't afford them. How can I ever pay him back?"

"Did he say you must pay him back?"

"We haven't actually got around to discussing it yet."

"Why do you anticipate trouble that may never come?"

"Whether he ever asks me to pay him back or not, I feel that I have to." Cammy searched for a way to explain. "Your people are proud, Miss Blackraven. Can't you see that it hurts my pride to accept help when I have no way of returning the favor?"

Talese looked at her in silence for a moment before she finally said, "Among my people there is a saying that you would do well to think about. 'We have all been warmed by fires we did not build.'"

As if that settled the matter, again the Native American appeared ready to shut the door and go, but Cammy stopped her with another question. "Do you mean that I should stay here and let Adam help me?"

Impatience flickered in the woman's black eyes, but otherwise her chiseled features remained stoic. "What I mean is that one day you may know the privilege of watching someone else enjoy your fire. But only if you *have* a fire."

This time the door clicked shut before Cammy could respond, and she was left alone to consider Talese's philosophy. There was a certain comfort in the reminder that Cammy wasn't the first to be down and out.

But, she thought gloomily, she seemed to find herself in that humble position more consistently than anyone else she knew. It would make for a pleasant change to be independent, a feat she could only expect to accomplish if she got a decent job and started supporting herself. And in order to do *that,* she must first accept more help....

Cammy dozed off at last, still analyzing the vicious circle in which she seemed to be trapped. Her sleep was restless, dream-filled, and every frame of her dream focused on a mysterious dark man who she recognized as Adam. Even in her sleep, her nerves tingled and her heart contracted with a painful kind of joy just to look at him.

The man was alone. Always alone. Nobody ever went near him, and when Cammy tried, he moved farther away from her. For every step that she took toward him, he took one backward, as if he didn't want her coming close. Yet he kept calling out to her in his low, husky, soul-stirring voice: "Cammy…Camelia Anderson…please don't go!"

Everything would be all right if she could just touch him, she thought. Just the slightest contact…just to have his lips brush lightly across hers. To get close enough to breathe in his familiar scent.

But always, always, he moved away from her, staying just beyond her reach. Cammy had never known her dreams to be so frustrating. Nor so *tantalizing*.

And then abruptly the dreams changed, taking on a nightmare quality when she discovered she and Adam were standing together in the middle of a burning house, with smoke all around and flames shooting up between them. He reached out for her as though to save her, but they were drifting farther apart, and she knew she would die if he didn't pull her out of the fire. Then she saw the tongues of flame grab him. Suddenly he was ablaze and she realized it was Adam who was going to die.…

She awoke sobbing and lay for a long time trying to rid her mind of the terrifying images. Her relief that it had just been a dream was overshadowed by her anguish at the possibility of something—*anything*—hurting Adam. Losing Gran had been hard, but Cammy literally shook all over at the thought of Adam's dying. She told herself he was young—only thirty-two years old—much too young to die. But he'd nearly died once already. His scars, though faded now, offered mute testimony to that fact.

It did absolutely no good for Cammy to argue with herself that she had no right to get so worked up over Adam's fate. True, except for the night he saved her from the fire, he'd never touched her. He'd never kissed her, never claimed to love her. But how she felt about him was another matter. She'd adored him from afar ever since she was a young girl; his unfailing kindness to Gran, and thus to her, had made him Cammy's knight in shining armor.

Her dreams tonight had served to remind her that Adam Neil was much too deeply entrenched in her subconscious to ever be ousted by mere common sense or logic. The fact that he didn't really care anything about Cammy personally couldn't stop her from caring about him.

"Say it, Cammy," she ordered herself aloud in the darkness of Adam's guest bedroom. "You're crazy about him. If he ever kissed you, you would fall head over heels in love with that man. You already want to marry him."

She sighed. She must be crazy, period. Because it was true; it would only take a kiss, a certain look, a single word from Adam and her heart would be his forever.

And yes, she did want to marry him. He had asked her for his own unknown reasons, and she was suddenly sure she could never in a million years say no to him. Even though he didn't love her. Even though she feared his past had so deeply embittered him that he would never be able to love *anyone*.

Who knows, maybe marriage would change him, chip away at his stony cynicism until it crumbled. Maybe it would soften him up by providing him with whatever had been missing from his life so far.

Adam . . . grow soft? Become magically transformed by her love? Not very likely! But what the heck? Feeling reckless, Cammy told herself it was high time she took a risk or two.

Chapter Six

Getting back to sleep was impossible once Cammy reached the decision. Suddenly eager for daylight, she stole out of bed and took all of her new cosmetics and beauty aids into the elegant dressing room that connected her bedroom to the bath. There, beneath the vanity lights, she spread out the assortment on the marble countertop and sat before the huge mirror to read the instructions on each container.

For the next two hours she practiced styling her hair with the curling iron, then applying makeup base and mascara, and finally eye shadows and blushers in an array of shades. She still hadn't achieved satisfying results when she noticed faint, distant sounds within the big house, which told her someone else was up and stirring.

Electrified, Cammy shed the brand-new white silk nightgown that had been among Adam's purchases and ran to the closet, where she sorted quickly through the clothes. Nothing that she saw looked as comfortable as her favorite jeans and cotton shirts that had been destroyed in the fire. But she supposed that would work out for the best. Jeans wouldn't make a suitable costume for what she planned to do.

Moving with haste, she stepped into a lovely dress in a pale blue-and-peach floral polished cotton, with a lace-edged collar and puffy sleeves and the kind of fitted waistline that complemented her slender figure. By the time she'd managed to zip it up the back and slip her feet into flats made of soft white leather, she heard an automobile engine starting nearby. Adam must be leaving for work!

Cammy's heart raced as she tore out of the bedroom and down the hall to the front entryway. Flinging open the door, she rushed out onto the verandah just as Adam backed his gray car out of the garage and around the side of the house.

Cammy called out his name in frustration, not really expecting him to hear, but to her surprise he braked the car and turned his head to look at her. She saw then that the driver's side window was rolled down in the pleasant morning air, and she supposed she ought to be grateful for that. Instead, she felt the bevy of butterflies in her stomach kick up a wild fuss. She wished fervently that she had held off on this discussion until Adam arrived home this evening.

What I should have done is just waited until he brought up the subject, she thought.

A second later she went cold as the possibility struck her that he might not be planning to mention it again, ever. Maybe by this morning he'd changed his mind.

Cammy felt her face turn several shades of red as Adam got out of his car and crossed the smooth, verdant lawn toward her, immaculately dressed as always in a pale gray three-piece suit with a maroon-and-silver striped tie. He looked every inch the Harvard-educated attorney today, and she began to think she must have just imagined last night's incredible conversation.

If she could have sunk through the flagstone porch, she would have without hesitation. This was going to be humiliating!

"Yes, Cammy?" Adam said rather abruptly. He stopped a step below her on the sidewalk, yet still had to look down a bit at her five feet four inches. The way his smoky eyes were taking her face apart, he could hardly miss the fact that her makeup job was amateurish, but good manners must have kept him from mentioning that. "Was there something you needed?"

He was standing close enough that she could detect his after-shave, and the scent had its usual disconcerting impact on her. It took a moment for her to register his curt tone, and when she did her heart sunk lower.

Now that he'd finished looking her over, his face was as rigid and impatient as his voice, and she had the distinct impression he would rather not be standing there talking to her like this. "I ... uh, I thought ... are you leaving for work?" she managed lamely.

Curbing his impulse to turn his back to her, he slid his left hand into his pocket so he wouldn't reach up to shield that side of his face—a habit that he had to fight in bright sunlight, where he felt so mercilessly exposed.

"Yes, I'm on my way," he told Cammy. "I have to be in court in an hour."

"Oh." She looked flustered. "Well, then ... I'm sorry. Go ahead."

She would have escaped back into the house, but just then he caught her arm. "Why did you stop me, Cammy?"

"No reason," she muttered, her eyes downcast to avoid his keen gaze. "I made a mistake, that's all. We can talk when you get home tonight, or . . . or whenever."

The more embarrassed she grew, the more determined he became to learn what she had been about to tell him. He had an oddly discouraged feeling that she'd been all set to give him her answer to his marriage proposal. A turn-down, no doubt. And now she thought she would spare him for another twelve hours.

His well-shaped mouth tightened. "I'd rather talk right now, Cammy. What is it that you were going to say?"

She could see he wasn't going to make this easy for her. Not that there *was* any easy way to handle this. "It . . . it was about your . . . idea," she stammered.

"Yes?"

Oh, Lord! He sounded cool, almost angry. Cammy fidgeted and laced her fingers together. "Your idea that we should get married." As if he might not know exactly what idea she was referring to!

When he didn't respond at all to that, she was forced to lift her eyes and meet his. His dark face seemed more masklike than usual, the scarred side pale, the expression distant and frozen. "What about it?" he asked finally.

Just before she would have blurted an appeal for him to forget the whole thing, his look stabbed Cammy in the heart with a sharp reminder of her nightmare that he had been about to die. She remembered, too, her reaction to the dream. Did she want to spend even one more night in tears?

Throwing caution to the wind she said, "Yes!"

There was a pause. "Yes?" He sounded absolutely blank.

"You asked me to marry you, and my answer is yes."

Adam's nostrils flared as he caught his breath in something very much like shock. She had taken him off guard, better prepared for a refusal than an acceptance. He stood completely still, his eyes never leaving her face as he tried to figure whether she realized what she was saying with such a brave air.

Well, he didn't intend to talk some sense into her. There were plenty of others who would be glad to do that, given half a chance. She might be a bit naive for twenty-one, but Cammy was an adult, and she had the right to marry him or not, without undue pressure from anybody.

He ignored the inner voice that inquired sarcastically whether he thought the fact that she no longer had a home might fall under the category of undue pressure. After all, *he* hadn't burned her house down. He only wanted to help.

Still, that voice whispered, if she weren't in such dire financial straits, she wouldn't have just said yes to his proposal.

If she weren't in such straits, I wouldn't have asked her to marry me in the first place, he thought and ended the argument with his conscience.

"Good. You're doing the right thing...the best thing you can do under the circumstances." He spoke in a clipped voice, thinking rapidly as he did so. It was essential that she not see or talk to anyone who might influence her to change her mind. A word with Tally would take care of that, temporarily at least.

With a hand at her waist, Adam steered Cammy back inside, saying, "My business in court this morning should be finished in an hour. Why don't I take you somewhere for lunch?" Without giving her a chance to refuse, he added, "You look nice in that dress. I hope you won't change."

Her heart somersaulted at his compliment, and at his musky scent and the light touch of his hand on her back. The thought of going out to lunch with him thrilled her. The thought of *marrying* him was beyond her comprehension.

"If you like this dress, I'll wear it to lunch," she said, eager to please him.

He gave her his typically wry, one-sided smile, this time a preoccupied one, and drew back his hand. "I forgot to tell Tally something. I'll pick you up around eleven."

As she watched him head toward the kitchen, a giddy intoxicating feeling, a feeling that bordered on victorious, pulsed through her, and Cammy almost floated on air as she returned to her bedroom. She had actually done it! She'd told Adam she would marry him, and he hadn't retracted his proposal. One day soon—maybe in a week, maybe a month—she would become Mrs. Adam Neil!

She halted in front of the dressing-room mirror to study herself. It seemed to her that she had changed...that she wasn't quite as plain and colorless as she used to be. Perhaps it was the makeup. Perhaps it was the dress. Or maybe it was the anticipation sparkling in her eyes—the exhilaration at the prospect of finally getting to know a man who had fascinated her ever since she first discovered the intriguing difference between boys and girls.

When a momentary doubt flickered across her mind about the wisdom of what she was doing, and she wished once more for someone to talk this over with, it suddenly struck her that she had never valued anyone's advice more than Gran's. And she was very well acquainted with that dear lady's opinion of Adam. Gran would have been tickled to death that Cammy was going to marry him!

By ten o'clock Adam had concluded his courtroom work and had stopped in briefly with a request for the county clerk. From there he went to see the district judge, who was a longtime colleague. Judge Weathers assured him that he would be available at a moment's notice to help facilitate Adam's wedding plans.

Before he left the courthouse, Adam thought it prudent to have a word with Cammy's best friend. Yesterday morning, bubbling over with concern because Cammy had narrowly escaped the fire and had lost all her possessions, Margo had dropped everything to go shopping with him. She had, in fact, provided invaluable information about Cammy's sizes in everything from underwear to shoes and made sure he remembered to buy all the little incidentals she would need. She'd also insisted that Adam's own fashion selections, in terms of style and suitability for Cammy, couldn't be improved upon. It had gratified him to find Margo as determined as he was that Cammy not have to ask her cousins for anything.

But that had been a mission to clothe and shelter Cammy. This was something very different, and Adam felt compelled to sound out the young woman, to determine whether she would approve or not. What he would do if she didn't approve, he wasn't sure.

"Greetings, counselor," the plump, vivacious brunette said with a friendly grin when he approached her in the motor-vehicle registration section of the tax assessor's office. "This morning's session of 'Divorce Court' didn't take long, did it?" she teased him.

A shrug and a lopsided smile were Adam's only response as he set his leather attaché case on the counter and met her gaze squarely.

She didn't avoid looking at his face, as some people did, but stared right back with a searching directness. Evidently something she saw in his expression puzzled her. "How's Cammy today?" she asked, suddenly anxious.

"She seemed fine when I saw her." Adam reminded himself that he was wasting time—time he didn't have—and he determined to get right to the point. Either Margo would help, or she wouldn't.

Leaning an elbow on the counter, he glanced around and saw that for the moment the large room was otherwise empty of staff and customers. He turned back to Cammy's friend and spoke in a low voice, aware that his news would probably stagger her. "I thought you might be interested to know that Cammy and I are getting married. If you can make it, I believe it would be good for her to have you at the wedding."

Adam had expected questions, even arguments. He hadn't expected Margo's joyous whoop or the enthusiastic hug that she twirled around the counter to bestow on him. "When?" she demanded. "And what can I do to help?"

A bit staggered himself, he went back to his office and had Maggie clear his calendar for the rest of the day. Among his messages, most of which he put aside for later, he found a note to call Freeman Burke. Adam deliberated a minute before reaching for the telephone and dialing.

"Hey, Adam!" Freeman's pleasant bass registered its usual warmth in greeting. "Glad you got back to me. Katie asked me to call and make sure you're coming this weekend."

Adam ran a hand through his hair in dismay. In the past few days' upset, he'd completely forgotten the Burkes' invitation. His silence alerted Freeman, who cautioned him, "Listen, buddy, don't even think of trying to get out of it. It's our wedding anniversary, you know." He chuckled. "The big one. Six whole months."

Adam sighed at the timing of things. "I'm sorry, but something's come up, and I can't make it."

"You have to make it," his friend said lightly, yet firmly. He'd dealt with Adam's reclusiveness before. "You were my best man. Katie won't even let me in the house if you don't come."

Adam smiled to himself. He knew better than to buy the other man's blarney. "I really am sorry, Freeman." He hesitated, then said, "Maybe Katie will forgive both of us if you tell her I can't come because I'm getting married."

"You're *what?*" Adam repeated it, and Freeman whistled. "Are you pulling my leg? Who are you marrying?"

"You don't know her. One of my clients...a neighbor."

His college and law-school comrade considered that. "Have you known her long?"

"All her life. Her grandmother and my mother were good friends."

"Well, hallelujah!" Freeman muttered, having evidently decided that this news called for a jubilant response. "When does this hitching take place? Katie and I will be there."

"You'd better hurry, then. It's set for noon today."

"Noon! Do you realize—" Freeman stopped shouting and collected his poise. "Where's it going to be?" he asked with resignation.

"I'm not sure. The courthouse, probably, but you'll never make it from Dallas in time, so don't even try."

"So give us a little more time. Hold off until two."

"I can't." He had no idea how long he could keep Lance at bay, once word of the pending marriage got out.

"Hmph. So this is how you treat your best friend?"

Adam paused, then heaved another sigh. "One o'clock. That's the latest I can manage. If you can't get here by one, stay home. I don't want you and Katie smashing up on the way to my wedding, do you hear me, Freeman?''

Returning home to pick up Cammy, he wished he had made it clear to Freeman that this wedding was no big deal. *Too late now,* he thought and consoled himself with the probability that the Burkes wouldn't be able to come.

Cammy was waiting for him, and on the drive back to town he saw that she'd removed most of her makeup and reapplied a toned-down, softer version. She kept throwing him hesitant, self-conscious smiles that made her look sweet and young. That made Adam feel old, and the tension that contracted every muscle below his chest as he watched her made him feel something of a lecher as well.

"Did you have a busy morning?" he asked abruptly, wondering if Lance had tried to get in touch with her today. Aware that several friends had called her yesterday while she slept, he'd instructed his housekeeper not to put through their calls today, nor to admit any visitors.

"No. I wanted to help Miss Blackraven clean house or something, but she had to keep answering the telephone. I just seemed to be in her way so I went to my room and looked at magazines until you came."

"Tally doesn't think she needs any help cleaning house." Seeing Cammy bite her lip, he added, "I'll tell you what . . . there's a small bedroom next to yours that can be converted into a work studio for you if you like. Your grandmother once told me that you enjoy making quilts."

"Oh, Adam, that would be wonderful!" With shining grateful eyes she studied his dark profile. The first quilt she made would be for him, for his bed.

Thinking about Adam's bed evoked all kinds of images she'd never dared to dwell on before and kept her too distracted to make small talk with him. Her cheeks still felt warm as Adam pulled his sleek car into the parking lot at the county courthouse and switched off the motor.

"Do you have some business to finish before lunch?" she asked. "I don't mind waiting in the car."

As he turned to her, his face took on the determined look she knew so well. "No, Cammy, you'll need to come inside with me. We're going to get our marriage license in the county clerk's office."

Her pulse fluttered in her throat. *"Today?"*

He nodded. "I've already asked them to look up your birth certificate, since proof of age is required. Once we have the license, we'll take it to the district judge and ask him to waive the usual seventy-two-hour waiting period."

Cammy's heart had begun jumping around in her chest, slamming noisily against her ribs. "You don't want to wait? Not even three days?"

"There's no reason to wait," he pointed out evenly. "It's not as if we need time to plan a big wedding. After Judge Weathers signs the waiver, he can perform the ceremony, or if he's busy, we can ask Tom Dillard to do it."

"Get married today...by the justice of the peace?" The question came out in an astonished whisper.

"It will be perfectly legal, Cammy," Adam said, wishing she wouldn't look at him like that, with stricken eyes.

"Yes, but..."

Here it came, he thought, steeling himself. When she just stared at him in miserable silence for a minute, her eyes welling with tears, he prompted her in a deadly quiet voice. "Yes but *what*, Cammy? Have you decided you don't want to marry me after all?"

Cammy's rushing, chaotic thoughts stalled abruptly, and she felt suddenly submerged in the perfect peace of knowing what she wanted. She wanted to marry him. But not in some fly-by-night ceremony by the justice of the peace.

She settled back against the seat and spoke with more assurance than she'd ever felt with this perplexing man. "I still intend to marry you, Adam, but not here. I want the minister to marry us. Jim Perkins buried both my grandparents, and your mother, too, in case you've forgotten, and he baptized me. Now he can marry us, in the church, where it should be done."

Adam knew better than to argue with Cammy over this. He only asked quietly, "What if he's not available today?"

She gave him a look of grave dignity. "He will be."

As it turned out, Cammy was right; Jim Perkins was available, and after a private word with Adam, the minister agreed to unite them in holy matrimony at one-thirty.

By that time Adam and Cammy had gotten all the paperwork out of the way and had informed Margo that the wedding had been moved to the church.

The sanctuary was bright from the sunlight streaming through the stained-glass windows and somewhat stuffy from the warm first-of-July day outside. There hadn't been time to order flowers, and the only guests present as the principals met at the altar were Margo Reese and Talese Blackraven.

"Dearly beloved," Jim said, "we are gathered here today in the sight of God—"

Suddenly the rear doors of the church burst open and several sets of footsteps hurried inside.

Adam swung around, his jaws and fists clenching at the possibility that Lance Anderson might try to stop the wedding.

Instead, a flood of intense relief washed over him when he saw Freeman Burke and his beautiful wife marching purposefully up the aisle. Katie slipped into the front pew next to Talese and Margo, while Freeman went straight to Adam's side.

"Can't very well have a wedding without a best man, can you?" he drawled.

Cammy had no idea who the tall, husky, laughing-eyed man could be, but she liked the look that had come over Adam's face. Turning, she called out, "Margo?" and beckoned her forward. If there was to be a best man, she should have a maid of honor.

Then she faced the minister again and announced with a calm authority that surprised those who knew her, "Now we can begin."

Chapter Seven

Adam eyed Cammy's almost untouched dinner plate, then her downcast face, with concern. "Is something wrong with your dinner?"

She looked up. "Oh, no! This roast beef is very good. I'm really grateful that Miss Blackraven fixed such a... such a delicious meal."

"Mmm...well, you're certainly not eating much. Since we never got around to having lunch, you ought to be starved."

Poking at her potatoes with her fork, Cammy ordered herself to start eating. "We've had a busy day, what with getting married and spending the afternoon visiting with your friends from Dallas. I guess I'm still a little—" she searched for the right word "—dazed. I never expected anyone to arrive at our wedding in a helicopter!"

"As Freeman explained, that was the only way they could get here on time."

"Still . . ." She shrugged, unable to tell him it was more than the Burkes' mode of transportation that had h nerves wound up tight; she had been unable to stop w dering what would happen at bedtime. Where w going to sleep tonight? Exactly what had he said b that topic?

Adam's mouth twisted into one of his self-m smiles. "It hasn't been your ordinary r Wednesday, has it? But cheer up. The wor

Her delicate brows drew together. Wh that? She wished she could ask him, leery of his answer.

"It hasn't been a *bad* day, Adam like the Burkes. They seem so ni

"Oh, yes, they're kind." But his didn't look especially pleased by her re the words were being dragged out again added, "Freeman has always been an exceptio soul. I met him as an undergraduate at Harvard. both sophomores, about nineteen years old."

Cammy tried hard to imagine Adam at nineteen but couldn't. She gave up and prodded him. "So when he married Katie six months ago, you were best man at his wedding?"

"Only because he wouldn't take no for an answer."

"You mean you didn't want to be in his wedding?"

Adam concentrated his gaze on the arrangement of pink and crimson roses in the center of the table, picking his words with care. "He's the best friend I've ever had. Nevertheless . . . I'm not a very social person, Cammy." He raised smoky, somber eyes to meet hers. "That's no surprise to you, is it?"

She shook her head, not knowing what to say.

"Then I hope you won't expect too much in that department." He sounded relieved.

"Were you worried about that?" Cammy couldn't help laughing. "I don't believe anybody in Comanche would describe me as a gadabout, Adam! I've spent most of my life on a farm. Singing in the church choir and going out to eat once in a while at the Continental Café are about the extent of my socializing. In fact—"

She broke off when the doorbell chimed a melodious interruption. A second later Tally marched through from the kitchen, mumbling under her breath and casting an uneasy glance back at the newlyweds as she cut a stately path across the living room, toward the front hallway.

An impish giggle escaped before Cammy could smother it. "Now *there's* someone you surprised."

"Who...Tally?" Adam arched one eyebrow in a way that signified disdain. "You don't know how to read her. It's not likely you'll ever take Tally by surprise."

Secretly Cammy wondered, but she couldn't pursue the subject since Tally reappeared just then to announce that "the young miss" had company.

"Who is it?" Adam asked, although he could have made a fairly accurate guess just from the housekeeper's disapproving expression.

"Mrs. Tucker."

Cammy wasn't used to hearing her cousin referred to like that, so it took her a moment to realize who Tally meant. "Babette's here?" she exclaimed. She pushed back her chair, half standing, and barely caught her white linen napkin before it slid off her lap. Laying the starched cloth on her seat, she straightened. "Where is she?"

"Outside on the verandah," Tally said without remorse. "I told her you were eating."

"I guess I'm finished." Cammy looked uncertainly at Adam. "I'd better see her."

"We'll both see her." He got to his feet, too.

"She probably didn't like having to wait outside," Cammy said.

Adam figured it wouldn't have made any difference where Cammy's cousin had waited; she probably wasn't going to be very happy over the news of the wedding.

It turned out he was right—Babette was all primed for a fight. The tall, buxom blonde sailed into the living room with blue eyes flashing and chin out. When she came face-to-face with Adam and Cammy, she ground to a scowling halt.

"It's good to see you—" Cammy began.

Babette turned to her dramatically. "I heard the most awful rumor today, Cammy. I came straight here so you can tell me yourself it's not true!"

Cammy knew her face was pink, but she attempted a smile. "If you heard that Adam and I got married, it *is* true."

At that, Adam moved closer to her side, to provide moral support, she figured. Out of the blue, he slid an arm around her waist. When she breathed in his irresistible scent and felt his lean, solid warmth brush against her, excitement began to bubble along her bloodstream like champagne suddenly freed from a bottle. Joy spun through her in a dizzying whirlwind, and she swayed a bit. Adam's arm tightened on her.

With difficulty she tore her attention from him and recalled her new role as hostess. "Would you like to sit down, Babette? We haven't had much chance to talk lately, so maybe..."

"No, I would not like to sit down. What in the world were you thinking of, to marry this man? Have you lost what little sense you started out with?"

With each brutal stab of her cousin's tongue, Cammy's happiness seemed to shrink and she felt her flush deepen, but she only said, "It's done, so I don't think there's anything to be gained from arguing about it now." Determined to be gracious, she stiffened her spine and said, "Miss Blackraven baked a cake today, and we were just about to have dessert. Will you join us?"

"For all you know she probably put poison in it!"

Watching, Adam marveled that anyone so crude and cruel could have descended from the genteel Louella Anderson, or be related by blood to Cammy, who was as sensitive, as well-bred as her grandmother had been. Then he chided himself. He should have learned by now that families, his own first and foremost, usually encompassed both good and evil.

"Babette!" Cammy protested. She had never seen her cousin act like this. But then she had never before crossed Babette, who showed only her sweet and charming side as long as she got her own way. "That's a terrible thing to say about a person."

Babette shook her head, full of righteous disgust. "You are such a fool, Cammy, you don't know the first thing about people! And you don't have any intention of doing what the rest of us want, do you? Why should you when you've just found yourself a permanent meal ticket? Fancy clothes, a big house, no more worries about working...you've sold out your own family for the easy life. When I think of all we've done for you...all *I've* done for you!"

Adam removed his arm from around Cammy and took Babette's elbow, firmly escorting her toward the front hallway. "You're not going to talk to Cammy that way in this house." His face and voice were hard as steel. "If you don't want to act civilized, you'll have to leave. Don't come back until you can control yourself."

"Come back? Ha!" She glared over her shoulder at Cammy, who followed in miserable silence a few steps behind. "You won't see me again until you apologize, Camelia Anderson. Not until you make things right for me and Lance and Joe Kenneth. You really think you've got it made, don't you?" There was spite in her laugh. "You'll find out soon enough what people think of you for marrying this...this monster." Flinging a hateful look at Adam, she shook off his hand. "Why do you think he was available anyway—this rich, big-shot lawyer here? Any woman in her right mind would be afraid to marry a man who killed his own brother. Not to mention all his scars—"

The next moment she was out the door and Adam was closing it behind her, his entire body gripped by a tremor of anger laced with pain. He hesitated with his hand on the doorknob, drawing in several deep breaths before he turned back to Cammy. "I have to go to the office," he said abruptly, his expression tight. "I didn't get much work done today, and some things can't wait."

He had started to move past her down the hall when she said, "Adam—"

"I'm sorry for abandoning you on our wedding night." The irony was heavy in his voice. "There's no telling when I'll finish, so do whatever you like this evening to amuse yourself. I'll probably see you tomorrow."

He would *probably* see her tomorrow? Stunned, Cammy blurted, "But, Adam—"

Not stopping to hear the rest, he strode through the house to the garage and left without another word to anyone.

Only later, as he paced like a caged tiger around his dark office that overlooked the deserted town square, only then did he let himself remember that there had been tears glittering in her eyes and a stricken look on her pale face as she appealed to him. He asked himself what she must have been feeling. Her family was no longer there for her. She had nobody...nobody except him. And Lord help her, he was no prize!

Weighted down with a sense of emptiness, Cammy fell asleep listening for Adam to return. The next morning at breakfast she learned that he hadn't come back the night before. Talese Blackraven refused to look at Cammy as she informed her that she had no idea where he might have spent the night. Cammy suspected that Talese blamed her.

For that matter, remembering the horrible, cutting things her cousin had said to him, Cammy blamed herself. No man should have to put up with such insults in his own home. If it hadn't been for her, Babette wouldn't have been there. Adam was probably wishing he had never involved himself in Cammy's problems. Maybe he was even planning to get out....

After a day spent moping about the house, she had just about prepared herself for Adam to spring an annulment on her the next time she saw him. It wouldn't have surprised her if he walked in at suppertime and ordered her to pack up and get out. Pack up *what,* she didn't know, because everything she owned had come from him. Nor did she have any idea where she would go....

Talese had warned her that on weekdays Adam liked to have dinner at six, so at five-thirty Cammy turned off the game show she was watching on the portable television set Tally had carted to her bedroom. She applied a modicum of makeup and tried to arrange her soft, fine brown hair into its usual pageboy, then inspected herself in the dressing-room mirror. Her eyes looked too big, and her mouth drooped perceptibly. There seemed to be no point in changing out of the loose-fitting white cotton sundress that was the simplest and most comfortable thing Adam had purchased for her. She looked all of sixteen years old in it, but so what? Adam probably wouldn't even show up.

Her first clue that she might be wrong came when she heard his voice as she approached the dining room.

First her pulse, then her feet sped up. Adam stood in the kitchen, leaning casually against the cabinet and talking to Talese as she emptied a pan of corn bread sticks into a basket to go on the table.

When Cammy entered, he turned his head and greeted her quietly, taking note of the bruised shadows beneath her eyes and her generally fragile appearance. Except for a tiny candle flame deep in her eyes, she looked desolate, which was understandable after the way Babette had lit into her last night. By now he supposed she must thoroughly regret having married such a "monster," as her cousin had put it.

So, Clark Kent, he thought dryly, *you performed your heroic gesture. You married her, provided her with a home, and guaranteed she wouldn't starve. Now what do you plan to do about her state of mind?*

One idea had been slowly taking shape, and as soon as he had seated her at the dinner table, Adam cleared his throat. "I thought this might be a good weekend to drive to Dallas. Freeman and Katie are celebrating their anniversary..." His voice trailed off when he saw Cammy's face. "You don't want to go, do you?"

"Me?" She looked stunned, then began to brighten at the realization that he apparently wasn't planning to dissolve their marriage. At least, not tonight. "You mean...I could go, too?"

"What did you think I meant?" He spoke gruffly. "I'm not the one who needs a new wardrobe, Cammy. Once you discover the joys of shopping in Dallas, I imagine we'll end up doing very little else while we're there."

"We don't have to go near a store if you don't want to," she assured him.

Adam accepted that with skepticism. It wasn't until the following afternoon, as they shot along the Interstate highway between Fort Worth and Dallas, that he began to suspect she had been sincere. "The Six Flags Mall is just ahead," he informed her, checking the clock on the dashboard of his luxurious car. "We still have three hours before we have to claim our reservations at the hotel. Do you want to stop here and take a look around?"

"Whatever you like." But she didn't sound very enthusiastic.

"You need some sports clothes," he reminded her. "You don't even own a pair of blue jeans, and that's unacceptable for a young lady from Comanche."

She ran a hand through her tousled hair, trying to undo the damage from the short nap she'd taken as he drove. "I won't be wearing jeans tonight, will I?"

"No, we have tickets to a play. I guess our first priority should be finding something you can wear to the theater."

Cammy watched his dark, reserved profile, anxious not to give him any reason to be ashamed of her. "Maybe you could drop me off at the hotel and go pick out something that you'd like me to wear. You know my sizes." Her small grin was hopeful. "At least, everything you bought the other day fits me."

"I had some help the first time." He looked perplexed. "You want me to go shopping for you by myself?"

"Shopping's never been one of my talents. Besides—" she gestured at her hair with an apologetic grimace "—if I'm going to look decent tonight, it may take several hours in front of a mirror. I haven't yet mastered all those cosmetics and things you and Margo picked out."

While Adam mulled over that in silence, Cammy noticed that they had sailed right past the Six Flags amusement park and past the mall bearing its name. A mile or so farther, he appeared to reach a decision. Accelerating, he sped on toward Dallas.

They ended up at what Cammy figured must have been the largest and most impressive shopping mall in the entire world. "Relax," Adam cautioned her when he saw her expression. "I just had an idea."

He found a parking place and they headed for the nearest department store. Cammy gazed around in awe as they entered the vast, glittering wonderland.

Grinning to himself, Adam paused to scan the store directory, then took the escalator to the beauty salon. There, he requested and received an immediate conference with the top consultant, a woman in her forties who was so beautifully groomed that Cammy felt like a lost cause.

Adam wasted no time. "If my wife were to give you free rein to do a complete make over, what would you do to her?"

Cammy hoped she didn't look as wounded as she felt. Adam thought she needed a make over? She did, of course, but he didn't have to be so blunt about it! He didn't have to announce it to the world at large.

The beauty expert deliberated before answering and stole several looks at Adam even as she studied the proposed subject of the make over. Cammy could tell that she found Adam enormously attractive and wasn't at all bothered by the flaws on one side of his face. Wearing an ivory linen suit and conservatively checked shirt, he appeared to be in his element in these sophisticated surroundings.

Cammy, on the other hand, felt like a fish out of water. She could just imagine what the other woman must be thinking of her total lack of style, when suddenly the lady took her by surprise. "Frankly, Mr. Neil, I'd try not to change very much about Camelia. May I call you that, dear?" she asked, looking at Cammy.

Cammy's mouth had fallen open at the news that this consultant didn't want to toss her out and start over from scratch. She closed her mouth and nodded with all the aplomb she could muster.

"You have such clear, fair skin...a nice contrast to your dark hair," the woman continued. "I wouldn't want to spoil your fresh, youthful appeal. I would introduce you to some softer peach shades of makeup, because the tones you're wearing now are a bit too harsh for you. I'd shape your hair and trim it shorter, choosing a style that you can maintain by simply washing it and blowing it dry. You look like you've got more interesting things to do than spend hours in front of the mirror every day." And she cast another sidelong glance at Adam.

When Cammy nodded, the woman turned to Adam for his approval. He asked, "How long will it take you to do all that?"

"Two hours at the most. You're welcome to sit in."

Cammy was glad when he said he would return later. The idea of his watching while someone made her over gave new meaning to the concept of butterflies in the stomach. They might have been neighbors all her life—they might even be married, by some inconceivable miracle—but they didn't know each other very well at all.

And that may never change, she thought, recalling the way he had sent her off to bed the night before with a calm, almost brotherly "good night."

She wondered what would happen at the hotel tonight.

Probably nothing, she told herself glumly. He had only married her out of the kindness of his heart, and she had better keep that in mind before she made a complete fool of herself.

Chapter Eight

Off and on throughout the performance that evening, Cammy gave herself a vigorous mental shake to make sure she wasn't dreaming. Her mind kept wandering so she really had no idea what was going on onstage.

She kept thinking how fantastic the day had been—how far removed from her old life! The refreshing, soothing beauty treatment she'd undergone at the hands of experts. The way she had looked afterward, like a delicate flower budding into full bloom. Adam's attentiveness since then. This dress she was wearing—a tea-length gown of Valenciennes lace panels over a pale blue sheath...the most beautiful creation she'd ever seen and undoubtedly worth a small fortune. The fact that the trunk of Adam's car was crammed with new clothes and accessories, all for her.

"Adam, you shouldn't have bought so much!" she had protested, stunned at the sight of all those boxes and bags. "Did you go hog-wild?"

"I've discovered that I enjoy buying things for you," Adam had responded. Suddenly the right side of his mouth curved up in a grin that could almost be described as playful. "You should have gone shopping with me if you wanted to have a say in what I bought."

The truth was, he had been astounded to find himself going from lingerie department to evening-wear salon to shoe store in search of just the right selections for Cammy. He had definite ideas about what suited her. *Proprietary* ideas. Cammy was his wife, and he wanted her to shine.

And shine she did. She looked lovely tonight. Both Katie and Freeman had remarked on it. He'd caught other men expressing it with their glances, and pride had swelled up inside him. Pride...the one major chink in his armor.

During the play he noticed her inattention and wished he had gotten tickets to a musical or a comedy, something she might have enjoyed more than this drama. Lately his mind turned more and more to pleasing her. When had that started? And was it just his imagination that he was growing overly preoccupied with her slim lithe figure... the petal-soft texture of her skin...the sweet fragrance that trailed after her...?

By the time the final curtain descended, Adam was as distracted as Cammy. When Freeman suggested that they go out for a late supper, he consented halfheartedly, thinking that Cammy deserved the chance to shine for someone other than just him.

The Burkes wanted to introduce Adam and Cammy to their favorite Italian restaurant, a small, out-of-the-way place. "We'll be dining in high style tomorrow evening. Tonight you'll have to settle for the real us," Freeman told Cammy, laughing but not really apologizing. "This place doesn't even serve alcohol."

"That's okay, I don't drink," she blurted, then wondered if Adam would have preferred that she keep that provincial fact to herself. His expression didn't tell her what he was thinking.

Conversing with Freeman and Katie proved fun. They were down-to-earth individuals with an obvious affection for Adam, and thus, a predisposition to like Adam's wife. Two days earlier at the wedding, Cammy had sensed a trace of polite reservation on Katie's part, as if she wasn't sure Cammy would prove worthy of Adam, but now both had evidently made up their minds that Cammy was perfect.

"I suppose you folks would rather proceed with your honeymoon than come over to our house for a while?" Freeman asked as they left the restaurant and strolled through the warm summer night, the lights of Dallas twinkling all around them. He held Katie close to his side, demonstrating that the honeymoon wasn't over yet for the Burkes.

"We really need to get back to the hotel." Adam gazed at the distant skyline as he spoke. "If we don't get some sleep, none of us will be worth much tomorrow."

"Sleep...uh-huh!" The other man chortled wickedly and gave his wife a loud kiss before unlocking the car door for his guests. "I'll just bet you plan to sleep."

"Freeman!" Katie hushed him. "Don't embarrass them."

Not certain how to respond, Cammy took her cue from Adam and smiled without answering. It was too bad Adam's friends had misread his reasons for marrying her. The mistake, although natural, must make it terribly awkward for Adam. Still, she would have thought he would've anticipated such a reaction and planned how to handle it.

The drive was quiet and their good-nights brief at the main entry of the hotel. Cammy yawned widely as she and Adam rode up in the elevator alone, and although he didn't remark on it, his mouth quirked as if he had started to say something.

Inside their suite, he stood silently watching her place her small pearl-studded handbag on the dresser. When Cammy glanced up, his darkly handsome image jolted her, searing itself deep in her heart and making her breath catch in her throat. He was so tall and erect, so heart-stoppingly masculine in his evening clothes! The knowledge that he was her husband sent shock waves crashing over her. That fact alone had to be the most unbelievable part of this whole adventure.

Then she looked into his smoky eyes and found an expression she'd never seen there before...one she couldn't decipher. Watchful, stormy, and possessing other mysterious qualities as well, that almost-haunted look tugged at her, drew her closer. As if her body had a will of its own, Cammy moved to face him and reached up to touch her palm to his cheek. "Adam, thank you—"

He pulled back fractionally, just enough to break the contact, and she felt the heat of mortification rush to her face at his rejection. Her hand dropped to her side. "Thank you for everything," she managed huskily. "It's been a...a wonderful evening. I'll see you in the morning." And she fled to the bathroom.

Adam winced as the door closed between them. *Cammy, I'm sorry!* he thought, his own hand covering the scars that she had touched so lightly. His withdrawal had been instinctive, an involuntary reaction to being touched there, but she'd acted as if he had slapped her.

With a heavy sigh, he turned and left her bedroom.

* * *

They returned to Comanche early Sunday afternoon, passing most of the trip in a silence that thankfully wasn't strained. For that matter, Cammy had shown no sign of hurt or embarrassment over Friday night's incident, and Adam thought maybe he had misread her reaction. She'd seemed her usual sweet self when he took her down to breakfast early Saturday morning and had remained that way through an outing to the Old City Park and the Dallas Zoo. Then Katie and Freeman had entertained them at home that afternoon, after which they'd dressed up and gone out to dinner.

Katie prepared an elegant Sunday morning brunch and invited an interesting assortment of a dozen other friends and neighbors, most of whom Adam knew from past stays with the Burkes. After eating and visiting awhile, Adam and Cammy left directly from there for Comanche.

"Almost home," she murmured as much to herself as to him, looking around with pleasure as they passed the Winchell dairy farm.

Adam heard an unfamiliar note in her voice and had to ask, "Will you be glad to get home?"

"Yes!" She couldn't wait to change out of her fancy dress-up clothes, put on one of the comfortably charming everyday dresses Adam had bought her, and set to work making a quilt. Although the Burkes were terrific, Cammy was tired of trying to act as if she always knew which fork to use.

Besides, Adam probably wouldn't feel he had to focus so much attention on her at home, and once she was alone, she could quit pretending that what happened Friday night hadn't just about killed her. Treating him as usual since her humiliation had been one of the most difficult challenges she'd ever met, and it hadn't helped to see the unspoken apology in his eyes that first morning. She couldn't stand for him to feel sorry for her.

Deliberately putting that out of her mind, she turned toward him and smiled. "Did you notice what I said? I guess I've already starting thinking of your place as home."

"It *is* your home."

She went on as if he hadn't spoken. "I need to do something about Gran's farm. I know I should go over and take a look…see if anything can be salvaged. But…" Her blue eyes clouded as she shook her head. "I don't even want to think about that house burned down, much less look at it."

He frowned. "There's no reason for you to look at it, Cammy. Some men from the fire department sorted through the debris as soon as the ashes cooled, and they assured me they found nothing worth saving."

"Still," she said doggedly, "I have to face it. I have to make myself go over there."

Adam's hands tightened on the steering wheel. He wasn't all that fond of viewing burned ruins himself, but she couldn't go alone. "All right, we'll drive over there soon, if you insist." If he put it off long enough, maybe she would change her mind. "As for your needing to 'do something' about the farm, there's no hurry. We've got a court date set to probate the will, and after that let's just take things as they come, shall we?" He changed the subject smoothly before she could reply. "You know, I had Pete Blanco bring your station wagon over to our place, and he said it died twice on the way. I think we need to get you a new car."

Cammy clicked her tongue as they turned into the driveway and parked in front of the house. "A new car?

Adam, that's really not necessary. It would be a lot cheaper to have the garage in town fix my Rambler."

"I don't want you driving something that may break down at any moment." His tone discouraged argument. "We'll go to the dealership tomorrow and see what they've got."

Cammy shuddered to think how deeply in debt to him she was getting, but it seemed that once Adam made up his mind about something, he flattened any obstacles in his path like a steamroller. The next day he came home for lunch, then took her back to Comanche to go car shopping, insisting that she test-drive several models on Leon Quincy's lot. Then when he selected a car that was so much fancier than anything Cammy had expected, she was left speechless. She had mentioned, half joking, that a red car would be nice, and since that color wasn't in stock, he ordered one with the stipulation that it be delivered within forty-eight hours.

It arrived from Fort Worth in less than twenty-four—a sporty red convertible. "To go with your new look," Adam said as he handed her the keys, a teasing reference to the fact that almost everyone in Comanche had noticed her make over the day before and commented on it.

"Oh, Adam!" They were standing on the front lawn in full view of Leon, who had driven the new car out from town, and Cammy acted without conscious thought. Repeating, "Oh, Adam, thank you!" she laced her arms around his neck and kissed him.

If she had stopped to remember where her last gesture of appreciation had gotten her, she never would have thrown herself at him so impulsively, and *certainly* not in front of an audience! He'd already made it clear he didn't care for any physical contact with her. The instant she realized what she was doing, Cammy froze, her heart going crazy as she waited for Adam to thrust her aside.

Instead, she heard his sharp inhalation...felt his taut stillness. She could even feel the staccato rhythm of his heart pounding close to hers where she pressed against his chest. Once again she had caught him off guard, but this time he managed to discipline his response.

A deep breath trembled through him and then his strong arms closed around Cammy. He took control of the kiss, his mouth moving over hers like a whisper of sweet promise.

Just as she grew aware of his hands on her back, just when her nerves were starting to melt from the compelling heat of his body molded against her, he hugged her one final time and released her. His mouth separated from hers with a languor that felt very much like regret.

Lifting his head, he stared down into her dazed eyes with an inscrutable look in his own. "My pleasure, Cammy," he said, his voice pitched low, yet loud enough for the car salesman to hear.

Mr. Quincy let out a rumbling chuckle. "Man, oh, man, Adam, I see now why you insisted on buying her the best. So would I, if she thanked me that way."

Adam smiled enigmatically. "Shopping for my wife does have its rewards."

If Cammy hadn't already experienced his rejection firsthand, she might have believed Adam was crazy about her. What a performance, she thought. Too bad that was all it was.

It had been effective, anyway, if Adam intended for the whole town to think he'd married Cammy out of love. When the men climbed into Adam's car and started back to the car lot, Leon Quincy was still grinning to himself over the scene he'd just witnessed. No doubt he would soon spread the word about Adam Neil's devotion to his new bride.

Of course, not everyone would believe it. And not everyone would rejoice at Cammy's good fortune, even if they bought Mr. Quincy's romantic little tale.

Suddenly the combination of her cousins' hostility and Adam's rigid self-sufficiency was more than she could cope with. Desperate to get away, Cammy jumped in her new car and inserted the key, then started the engine. It responded with a muted but powerful roar.

When Talese Blackraven stepped out onto the front porch and stood watching her, her broad forehead crinkled in a disapproving scowl, Cammy ignored the housekeeper and sped out of the driveway. Fighting tears, she turned onto the county road and headed south.

Tally reached Adam on his car phone just as he was parking at his office. He listened, then muttered something beneath his breath, and turned his car around.

He arrived at the Anderson farm a few minutes later and parked behind the red convertible. Cammy was sitting on the haystack where he'd carried her the night of the fire, hugging her knees and staring at the pile of black bricks, twisted appliances, and charred wood that had once been home.

Adam approached her slowly. Up close, he saw her anguished expression, and his heart took an unexpected twist. He clenched his jaw and sat down beside her, conscious of the ravaging sun overhead. Shrugging out of his coat, he laid it next to him on the straw and watched a cloud of dust puff up, then settle back onto it. He grunted. "This suit will never be the same again."

She didn't look at him. "Why'd you come?"

"Why did *you?*" he countered.

"I told you I had to."

"Couldn't you have waited and come with me one evening?"

"I didn't want to bother you."

"Well, what do you think you're doing?"

She turned at that, mouth trembling, blue eyes welling with tears, and before she could say a word, Adam grabbed her hand and held it tight. "Cammy, I'm sorry! I didn't mean that the way it sounded. I'm just..." He stopped, shook his head, and sighed. "You worry me."

"That's the last thing I want to do," she whispered, her gaze drawn to their entwined hands. He had actually reached for *her* this time. His warm, strong grip sent a tingle of electricity through her fingers and up her arm. She didn't want to tell him how miserable she'd been every time she thought of last Friday night. "I just came here to look things over and to... to think, I guess. Think about what I should do."

"Can't you think at home?"

She kept her eyes lowered. "That's just about all I ever do there, only it never gets me anywhere. I'm not used to being idle. Maybe I should start looking into some type of schooling."

"There's no hurry. I'll speak to Tally about your helping her. And I'll move the furniture out of that other bedroom tonight so you can begin quilting."

As he spoke, Adam watched her silky, downswept lashes and wondered what she found so fascinating. Following her gaze, he saw their fingers laced together and grimaced. In the sunlight, the skin on his hands was discolored and uneven, especially right next to her creamy smooth ones.

He started to release her, but she held on. Her fingers pressing his, she looked up at last. "I'd love to do some cooking, Adam.'' She gestured past him with her head, indicating the garden patch near the barn. ''I'm going to lose all my vegetables if I don't pick them soon.''

Adam was so glad to see her tears drying up, he would have agreed to almost anything. ''Why don't I help you?'' He stood. ''I imagine there are some buckets in the barn, aren't there?''

''You'll help me? Don't you have to get back to work?''

''It can wait.''

''But your clothes—''

Grinning crookedly, he flicked at a spot of dirt on his trousers. ''They seem to be past saving.''

She felt like throwing her arms around him again but restrained herself. ''Thank you, Adam.''

All too conscious of her hand in his, he answered quietly, ''You're welcome, Cammy.''

For the first time in Cammy's memory, Talese broke into a smile when she saw the washtubs full of garden produce that Cammy and Adam were carrying in. Corn on the cob, melons, black-eyed peas, beans, squash, okra, new potatoes, turnip greens, tomatoes, cucumbers, bell peppers—it was enough to daunt anyone else. Tally just kept muttering her approval as they lugged in container after container.

When Adam went to clean up and change clothes before heading back to the office, the woman remembered how to frown. ''Nobody could eat all this before it spoils. It should be canned.''

''That's what Gran and I always did, after we shared with the neighbors,'' Cammy said, hot and sweaty but happy. ''I'll help you.''

The wrinkles in Tally's forehead smoothed out, but only for a moment. "If I did not have supper to fix, we could begin now."

"Why don't you let me cook supper?" Cammy suggested. "You can go ahead and start canning."

When Tally hesitantly agreed, Cammy hurried to her room for a shower. Worried that Talese would change her mind, she barely took the time to slip into a shell sweater and slacks, then followed only the sketchiest version of the beauty consultant's expensive instructions before hurrying back to the kitchen.

There, she spent the rest of the afternoon trying to stay out of Tally's way as much as possible while preparing a dinner of Southern-fried chicken, mashed potatoes, and an array of other vegetables using recipes Gran had taught her. Adam's compliments and the warmth in his eyes amply rewarded her efforts.

After supper, the two of them labored together moving the furniture from the bedroom next to Cammy's, into the other guest rooms. They took the bed apart and stored it in the garage. Watching the flexing of Adam's back and shoulder muscles beneath his shirt as he hefted the mattress up into the rafters made Cammy sharply aware of his lean strength. His black hair ended up tousled and his face beaded with perspiration from the exertion, and she thought she'd never seen him look so appealing. It was hard to keep her mind on moving furniture.

"I'll need some long strips of lumber to make a new set of quilting frames," she said when everything that needed to go had been cleared out. "Gran's got burned up."

He put his hands on his hips and eyed her quizzically. "You think you can make your own frames?"

"Well, sure I can! Gran made hers. I just need some large screw clamps from the hardware store, and a hammer and tacks." She grinned impishly. "And, of course, a closet full of fabric scraps to make the quilts."

"I'll get the wood and the hardware for you, but I'm afraid I won't be much help in the scraps department."

"No problem," she said, waving one hand airily and leading the way to the kitchen to get some iced tea. "Margo's mother and several ladies at church have offered me their sewing remnants."

"That's good," he said absently, thinking how soft her mouth looked as she sipped her drink. Against his better judgment, he let himself recall that it *was* soft, and that her hand was fine-boned and infinitely tender....

He wrenched his gaze away from her and downed his iced tea in a couple of swallows. "I think I'll go to bed early. Good night, Cammy."

Her throat was suddenly so tight she couldn't answer as he left the room. Every time he went off to bed alone, it hurt her more. Telling herself she should be grateful for his friendship did no good. The ache of longing in her heart grew deeper each day, and there was only one thing that could satisfy it. And it *wasn't* friendship!

Chapter Nine

Cammy and Margo heaved the chock-full bushel basket out of the trunk of the convertible and carried it up to the porch of the Reese house. There they set it next to another container that also threatened to overflow with yield from the Anderson garden.

"Whew!" Margo wiped her forehead with her sleeve as she sank down onto the steps. "Mom said to tell you thanks, Cam. We really appreciate this. But next time how about picking the stuff before it gets so heavy?"

Glad for the shade, Cammy sat beside her and grinned. "I can't make any promises, but I'll try."

"Well, at least promise to bring your husband along when you deliver it."

Cammy's smile slipped at the mention of Adam. "To do the lifting, you mean?"

"That, too, but I really meant to provide a distraction as we work." Margo sighed. "I still can't believe it. You spend one night in his house and he marries you! And after all your talk about not lusting after him..."

It was Cammy's turn to sigh, but inwardly, so as not to disillusion the romantic Margo. Although she knew Margo would keep it to herself, Cammy couldn't bring herself to tell a soul that she was Adam's wife in name only.

"What's it like—married life? You've been living with him almost a month now."

As she carefully phrased her answer, Cammy rested her chin on her hand and stared at the highway that swept past Margo's front door. Finally she said, "Much more of it and I'll be spoiled. Adam's very good to me."

Truer words had never been spoken. Thanks to Adam, she spent her days doing the things she enjoyed most— looking after her garden back on Gran's farm, piecing quilts, and sometimes helping Tally with the cooking. As for cleaning house, Tally wouldn't permit her to lift a finger, despite Cammy's protests that she was going to grow lazy.

There had been no mention of her starting school; in fact, she was beginning to think Adam didn't particularly care if she ever went to school or got a job. He provided a generous allowance besides giving her everything she could possibly desire.

Make that *almost* everything. He never initiated any contact with her, instead treating her like a sister. At least he hadn't pulled back the few times she had got up her nerve to give him a sisterly peck on the cheek at bedtime.

And there were times... She shivered, thinking about the flood of feelings that swept through her when their hands accidentally touched or her eyes met his. It was...well, confusing was just about the best way to describe it. Joy and exhilaration and intense yearning and a sense of acute hopelessness seemed to fill her so full that there wasn't room for all of her emotions at once, yet the feelings were tangled into such a knot inside her that she couldn't separate them. At those times she could hardly breathe.

Margo was saying, "Any fool can see he's good to you. But is he, you know, *good?*" She wiggled her eyebrows meaningfully.

Cammy could feel her face turning ten shades of pink and couldn't think of an answer. She knew that only good manners prompted her best friend's next words. "Okay, okay, I withdraw the question." Margo scowled across the road at the city water tower. "Mom told me not to butt in, but I have to say this. No matter how crazy he was about me, I wouldn't let him go on working with that Magness woman if I were you."

"April Magness?" Cammy remembered that Margo had mentioned Adam's rich client once before. "I can't tell him who to represent, Margo."

"Why not?"

"I just can't. I don't interfere in his business."

"Hmph! I think she's got a lot more than business on her mind. Why would any woman possibly need to see her lawyer three times a week?"

"Are you sure she sees him that often?"

"She goes in every other day at the very least. From my window in the courthouse, I watch her drive up and park that big white Cadillac of hers and then flounce into his office. Sometimes she comes right back out and sometimes she doesn't. I guess it depends on whether Adam's there and how busy he is." Margo slapped at a gnat that was humming around her face and gave her friend a look of concern. "You *are* aware, aren't you, that April was wearing Colby Neil's school ring when he died?"

Cammy just shook her head numbly while her stomach gave an uneasy lurch. She could remember, as a kid, having heard rumors about rivalry over a girlfriend being the thing that triggered the...the...whatever had happened between Adam and his younger brother. Colby had died when Cammy was six, and in all the years since, the population of Comanche had never reached a consensus over who was responsible for his death.

There had been an official investigation, but nobody seemed to know the results, if any. A few locals still believed the fire was an accident. Some blamed the whole thing on a mean streak in Colby that had boomeranged, while others swore up and down that Adam had set out to kill his brother and had been inadvertently burned himself.

How anyone could believe that, Cammy couldn't imagine. But then, she reminded herself, nobody in Comanche had ever really known Adam very well, either before or after the fire. Both Colby and Adam had gone away to private schools from a relatively early age, and afterward...well, afterward Adam had kept to himself more than ever. And, of course, intermittent treatment for his injuries had followed, as well as college and law school in the East....

Whenever Cammy asked questions about the fire, Gran and Grandpa had forbidden her to pay any attention to or repeat the gossip, saying that the Neils were fine people, the salt of the earth despite their wealth, and that they'd suffered too much already. That answer had never completely satisfied Cammy, but it had to suffice since her grandparents held firm to the opinion that whatever had happened within the Neil family didn't concern the rest of the town.

Unfortunately for Adam, the rest of the town didn't necessarily share that opinion and still debated about it from time to time, usually in whispers and as often as not to Adam's detriment. In spite of the gossip, Adam's law practice always appeared to thrive, a fact that Cammy could only attribute to his reputation as a hardworking, competent attorney, just as his father had been.

"I don't think Adam gives two hoots for April," Margo went on darkly, "but she's been fascinated by him for years, and I doubt if she'll rest until she gets her claws into him. So it's up to you, pal, to stop her."

"In that case, we'd better start praying *hard,*" Cammy quipped. The suggestion that she could deter an experienced sexpot like April Magness struck her as a sick joke.

"Hey, I'm not worried. He married you, not April."

Somehow that didn't reassure Cammy, perhaps because she was remembering that April was already married, and to a much older man with a reported heart condition. How long was Raleigh Magness expected to live, anyway? And in anticipation of his demise, did April already have her next rich husband picked out?

Sitting in church the following Sunday morning, Cammy found herself pondering those same questions when she saw the coquettish redhead enter and take a prominent pew. April smiled at Adam as she passed him— a smile so fraught with familiarity that it made Cammy's blood simmer. The woman had never attended church until a few weeks ago!

But then Adam had seldom gone to church until after the wedding, and now he came with Cammy every Sunday. She guessed it must be his hyperactive sense of responsibility at work again. Oh, well. Whatever motivated him, she didn't plan to complain. It was far too pleasant having him beside her throughout the sermon, smelling like her own personal idea of heaven and looking quietly distinguished in suit and tie.

That started Cammy wondering, as Jim preached, whether Adam ever dressed casually. In the month since they got married, she'd seen him without his jacket, but never without a tie, not even after a steamy hot day in court when anyone else would have lounged around the house in cutoffs and a T-shirt. Maybe he actually slept in a necktie. Maybe she ought to sneak into his bedroom some night and find out. She grinned at the image of dark, lean Adam in bed, naked except for a somber black tie looped around his neck.

Feeling suddenly warm, not to mention more than a little guilty at the direction of her thoughts, Cammy sneaked a blushing look at Adam and found him watching her, too. He was clearly trying to figure out what had prompted her naughty grin, and as the organist began playing the final hymn, Cammy scrambled for something to tell him in case he asked. Something other than the truth.

She knew instinctively that he wouldn't like her to picture him undressed. That had to be at least part of the reason why he never shed his tie or unbuttoned his shirt around her. He felt safer keeping a barrier between them, so she wouldn't start imagining that she really knew him. He probably figured his clothed state would keep her from thinking intimate thoughts. If so, he underestimated his own appeal.

She was still pondering that as they walked to their car after the service ended, when suddenly Margo caught up to them. "Don't look now, folks, but trouble approacheth. If you hurry, you may get away before it strikes."

Sure enough, Lance was bearing down on them from the opposite end of the parking lot. But rather than get in the car and speed away, Adam stopped and waited, looking as if he wouldn't mind a confrontation.

The blond, smoothly handsome man ignored Adam and plunged into the fray without a civil word of greeting for his cousin. "How much longer do you plan to hold out on us, Cammy?" he demanded in a bold voice, evidently not caring who heard him. "Do you really think you can get away with cheating me and Joe Kenneth and Babette?"

Cammy saw to her chagrin that although Margo had tactfully vanished, several other people lingered nearby listening. She glanced at Adam, saw his clenched jaw, and then appealed to Lance. "Why don't you come over to the house so we can talk—"

"Are you ready to sell the farm?" he cut in rudely. "Because if you're not, there's nothing to talk about."

"Then as you said, we have nothing to talk about," Adam responded, opening the car door and taking Cammy's arm to help her in.

Lance grabbed Adam's shoulder as if to push him out of the way, but Adam spun around so quickly that Lance stumbled backward. The onlookers gasped.

"Keep your hands off me," Adam said, his voice quiet. "And watch what you say to my wife."

Lance made an obvious effort to regain his composure, but his complexion was growing redder by the minute. "This doesn't concern you, Neil," he muttered.

"Anything that concerns Cammy concerns me."

"Then you'd better convince her to sell the farm. She has no right to keep us from getting our inheritance. It's as much our land as it is hers, and we're in the majority. If the rest of us want to sell, she should sell."

"Have you checked with your attorney about that?" Adam asked almost pleasantly.

"Yeah, I have, and he says we can take you to court. We can sue the pants off you."

"George Biggs has his facts straight about one thing—you can sue anybody you like for anything. That doesn't mean you'll win. And in this case, you don't have a legal leg to stand on. You'll be wasting your time and money."

"You'd like me to believe that, wouldn't you?" Lance said bitterly.

"I don't care what you believe. It's the truth."

"Sure! Like you tried to make everyone believe I burned down my own grandmother's house. What do you say about that now?"

The rest of the audience had dispersed by then, probably out of sheer embarrassment. Adam shot a guarded look at his wife. Although he had never attempted to smear Lance's reputation, he hadn't gotten around to telling Cammy what he had learned from the fire chief last week, either. Right now he felt more disgusted with himself than guilty. What had he been afraid of, anyway?

Clearing his throat, he said, "There was no sign of arson. Apparently the fire was caused by a short in the electrical wiring."

"Yeah," Lance sneered, seeing Cammy's surprise as she gazed up at her husband from the front seat of the car. "So why should anyone take the word of a coward and a murderer, who also happens to be a liar?"

Intending to insulate her, Adam shut the door before Cammy had a chance to gasp out what she thought of such baloney. Through the car window she could still see the muscle jerking in his unscarred right cheek and hear a peculiar flat note in his voice as he said, "Why don't you go ahead and sue so we can find out who's right?"

"I plan to," Lance shouted as Adam circled the car to get in on the other side. "You can't throw your weight around with my family and get away with it, Neil! Cammy may be a fool, but when we haul her into court, she'll come to her senses soon enough and wish she'd never heard of you."

That was such a ridiculous threat, Cammy didn't bother remarking on it as they drove home. What worried her by that time was Adam's grim, stony-faced silence. She had seen him look like that before; it had been after Babette's harangue, the night of their wedding. He'd disappeared all night that time. Would he do so again?

Cammy wished she could muzzle her viper-tongued cousins. Anything to keep them from hurling any more insults at Adam.

If only she knew how to take away his hurt! But Adam always acted so self-contained, so completely self-reliant. He never shared what he was feeling, not even the good. Even his smiles seemed to hoard his pleasure, never stretching beyond a one-sided grin, never reaching his eyes.

As he stopped his car in front of the house, Cammy said with forced gaiety, "Tally was going to try a new dish for dinner today. I can't wait to taste it!"

When Adam pocketed his keys and got out, she breathed a sigh of relief that he planned to stay. But as he walked her up to the door, he flicked back his cuff and checked his wristwatch. "Apologize to her for me, will you? I'm not very hungry. I have a whole afternoon of work ahead of me, getting ready for court tomorrow."

Cammy took hold of his hand so tightly that he gave her a startled look. "You're not going to your office, are you?"

"No." Pulling his arm away, he reached up to rub the back of his neck. "I'll be in my study working."

Just inside the front door they parted. Cammy watched him head down the hall, his back as straight as ever, and wondered if she had only imagined the traces of pain in his eyes.

She shook her head, certain that Adam was suffering, and just as sure it was a side effect of his encounter with Lance. Knowing that he preferred to face it alone left her feeling wretched.

Although Talese had gone to a lot of trouble to prepare a new recipe, Cammy ate without enthusiasm. "You getting sick?" the housekeeper asked suspiciously.

Cammy denied it, wishing she could tell Tally how concerned she was about Adam, about the way her cousins had been treating him. But somehow she couldn't confide in the woman. Whenever the urge built up inside her, she kept picturing Tally staring down at her with scorn in those dark eyes and growling something that would put Cammy right in her place: *"Do not make yourself a bigger fool than you already are, missy. Adam is fine. He has always been fine. He does not need you to look after him."*

After lunch Cammy started to her room, but she paused outside the door to Adam's study. It was closed and probably locked. She knew better than to bother him when he worked, but just this once, no matter what Tally might say...

Very quietly, she opened the door. If he was engrossed in reading or paperwork, she planned to shut it again and go away, at least for a while. Then later she would take a tray of food to him and try to persuade him to eat.

But Adam wasn't working. Instead, the window shades were drawn, and in the dimness she could see him stretched out on his back on the blue sofa, a forearm covering his eyes. He'd removed his suit coat and tie and tossed them onto the arm of a chair, and he had undone the top button of his shirt before lying down.

Slowly she approached, trying to determine if he was asleep. When she stood over him, she could hear the uneven sound of his breathing through slightly parted lips ... distinguish the faint rise and fall of his chest ... see his whitened knuckles against the darkness of his clenched fist.

Cammy knelt beside the sofa and carefully slid one hand beneath the arm that rested across his face, whispering his name at the same time. "Adam ... Adam, it's Cammy." She felt his entire body tense up and heard him suck in his breath, but his arm stayed rigidly in place. "I didn't mean to startle you." Her voice, soft and soothing as velvet, coaxed him to relax. Taking a guess, she asked, "Does your head hurt?"

After a long moment he lowered his arm and looked at her. She was close—too close—but it was so nearly dark in the room that he didn't try to move. Her hand was stroking his forehead, and almost against his will he closed his eyes and nodded. He would have admitted to just about anything as long as she kept that up. Besides, it was true: he had a world-class headache.

Cammy threaded her fingers into his hair, intending only to relieve his pain. But when the thick black silk brushed across her naked palm, it kindled a sweet and fiery meltdown deep inside her. Her heart responded with a silent cry of anguish. Dear Lord, she loved him! Why couldn't she always caress him like this?

For interminable minutes she stayed there on her knees, one hand gently massaging his scalp and forehead and temples, the other resting on his chest. Tears of frustration pricked her eyes as she gazed at Adam, but she didn't dare let her feelings go. Not when he might see her crying! She couldn't possibly explain her tears to him.

Some time later he opened his eyes again and gave her a vaguely troubled look, but all he said was, "Thank you, Cammy. It feels better now."

She didn't rise. "You're welcome." Her expression was
graver than usual, her blue eyes wide. "It was the least I
could do since it was my family who gave you the headache." Biting her lip, she unconsciously twisted her fingers into his shirt.

When her hand slipped between the buttons and grazed
the skin of his chest, he caught it and extracted it without
a word. Although there was nothing angry in his gesture,
it convinced her he didn't want her touching him. She
wouldn't blame him if he hated her for all the trouble she'd
brought on him. This time when the tears filmed her eyes,
she didn't bother hiding them. "I just wish I could make
up for the way my cousins have been acting, Adam."

"It's not your fault." He was watching her closely, de-
bating whether now was the time to bring up a potentially
tricky subject. All she could do was say no...and perhaps accuse him of having a thirst for vengeance, which
was uncomfortably close to the truth. But Lance Anderson
had pushed him too far with his relentless campaign
against Cammy, and Adam wanted the other man to hurt
for a change. "There is one thing I'd like to ask of you."

"What?" She brightened immediately and her tears
vanished at the thought of pleasing him. "Just name it. I'll
do anything."

"You can lease your farm to Ted Nix." Seeing her confusion, he explained. "He told me the other day he needs
another couple of hundred acres for grazing, the way his
herd's been multiplying. Being able to use your place
would help him a lot."

She didn't even have to consider it. "Tell Mr. Nix he can
move his cows onto Gran's farm tomorrow."

Adam blinked, then raised his hand and curved it
against her cheek. He only meant to ask if she was sure, if
she could really be that sweet and agreeable; but instead,

something made him gently catch her by the nape and draw her facedown to his level. The instant her satin lips touched his, liquid lightning streaked through him in a flash of heat, leaving breathless chaos in its path. He wanted her so bad, his heart seemed to be trying to thunder its way up into his throat.

No. This wasn't going to work! This wasn't what he had intended to happen when he married her. Adam was no fool. He knew better than to let himself care like this. *Oh, God, don't let me lose control now,* he prayed.

He released her as if she had burned him, and she got to her feet, looking as thoroughly shaken as he felt. And looking, for some odd reason, guilty.

"I'd . . . I'd better go," she stammered, then turned and left the room before he could manage a reply.

Chapter Ten

Maggie Frost tapped at the open door of Adam's office, her purse strap slung over one shoulder. "Five o'clock, counselor. Time to go home."

He glanced up from the brief he'd been reviewing and motioned for her to go ahead. "I'll be through soon. See you tomorrow, Maggie."

"Oh, no you don't, Adam. None of this I'll-leave-in-a-minute business. You've worked late every night for the past two weeks."

"I won't stay late tonight."

"You're darn tootin', you won't. I'm not leaving until you put down that stuff and come with me. I want to watch you get in your car and drive off."

"I'm not quite finished," he said reasonably.

"Let it wait." The young woman stood tapping one foot, looking as if she couldn't curb all her energy. Adam figured she was itching to get to the tennis courts. She played the game daily, year in and year out, and both her figure and her complexion showed it.

He gave her an ironic half grin. "You do realize who's the boss around here, don't you?"

"I certainly should, considering how long I've had to put up with you," she muttered good-naturedly. "I also happen to know that what you're working on can wait until tomorrow morning." Her look changed, becoming level and serious. "If you keep up this pace, your sweet young wife may get the idea you don't want to come home to her."

Adam felt his stomach tighten and his grin fade. He could hardly tell Maggie why he put off going home just as long as possible. Not because he didn't want to spend time with Cammy but because he *did* want to so badly. Because he wanted to grab her and hold her close every time he saw her. Because he ached to steal into her bedroom at night and crawl beneath the bedclothes and lose himself in her fragrant sweetness. Because he would scare her to death if he acted on his wishes.

"Give the girl a break," Maggie went on, her freckled nose wrinkling persuasively. "This is a special day. She's probably got big plans."

Special? Adam started to suggest that that was a matter of opinion, but he only asked impatiently, "How would Cammy know what day this is?"

"You mean to say you didn't tell her?" His efficient, warm-hearted secretary lifted an eyebrow. "Shame on you, Adam Neil! Anyway, I'll bet Talese clued her in."

He wiped a hand down his face, hiding his sigh, and stood up. "You're probably right."

Just as he was locking the outer door, Maggie let fly with an uncharacteristic oath. "What timing! Shall I get rid of her for you?"

He saw the white Cadillac pull up then, and he sighed again. "No, that's all right. I'll handle it."

"You should be good at that by now. Why on earth—" Maggie stopped, then shrugged and started for her car.

"Thanks for lunch," Adam called after her.

"The pleasure was all mine," she hollered back, waving goodbye.

He walked slowly toward April Magness's car and bent his head near the driver's window when she rolled it down. "What brings you here? It's after five."

The smile that she beamed up at him was warm. "I wanted to wish you happy birthday."

He started to tell her it hadn't been necessary but knew she would argue about that. "Thanks."

"This is for you." She handed him a small gift-wrapped box from a jewelry store in Stephenville.

Adam took the package but didn't open it. This time he had to say it. "I wish you hadn't done this, April." When she just kept smiling, he added, "You know, I've told you it's not a very good idea for us to be seen together here."

"Climb in, then, and we can go for a drive."

"I don't think that's the solution," he said dryly. "Wherever we went, people would probably see us and talk."

She narrowed her heavily lashed eyes to study him. "It never used to bother you for people to talk."

Turning, he leaned against the car and stared across the street at the town square. There was ample traffic passing to guarantee that this tête-à-tête with April would make the rounds of the courthouse and café set tomorrow. "That was before. I'm married now."

"I was *always* married," she pointed out.

He looked back down at her, unsmiling. "I know."

"Well?" she pressed him.

"Well, nothing. I just don't want people gossiping now." He tried to give the present back to her, and when she refused to take it, he shook his head in exasperation. "Look, April, I don't know how Raleigh would feel about your spending his money on an expensive gift for another man, but I know how I feel. Lousy."

"You're not just another man, Adam," she said so quietly that he realized his sharp words had hurt her. "You're a very special friend. At least I thought you were my friend."

He hunched his shoulders and stared at his feet. "Of course. But I don't want a present—"

"How can you know until you open it?"

When he sighed and started to tear off the bow, April stopped him rather urgently. "You'd better get in the car to do that. I mean, if you're worried about what people might think...."

Oh, Lord. Adam had a sinking feeling in his stomach as he went around and climbed in. "Why don't you just take this back and get something for yourself?"

"Absolutely not. Open it."

Reluctantly he did and found that his worst suspicions were well-founded. The jeweler's box held a 24-karat gold, diamond-encrusted ring. Adam looked at it, then raised his eyes and shook his head at her again. "I can't possibly accept this."

"You have to. It's a gift, given in the spirit of friendship, because I care so much about you."

"I appreciate the thought," he said, "but for me to take the ring would be misleading, not to mention a terrible waste, since I can never wear it."

"Why can't you?" April asked abjectly. "Because it's from me?"

"If you'll notice, I don't even wear a ring from my wife." He flattened his hand and held it out palm-down between them, showing her the blemished back of it. "Rings just attract attention that I don't need."

"Oh, Adam, don't!" Her voice breaking, she caught his fingers and pressed them to her mouth. "Don't keep hating me!"

"I don't hate you," he said and withdrew gently from her grasp. Snapping the ring box shut, he gave it back to her. "It's getting late. I'd better get home."

"If you refuse to keep the ring, I'll never believe you don't hate me. Besides, one day you may change your mind about jewelry."

"I doubt that." His mouth quirked, but he didn't stop her when she slipped the box into the pocket of his jacket as he was getting out of the car. He didn't want to waste the rest of the evening arguing with her. Suddenly the only thing that mattered was getting home to Cammy. "Let's call it even now, April," he said, and she gave him a long look without answering.

"I hear his car now," Cammy whispered to Tally. Whispering wasn't absolutely required, but she was too excited to care about that.

Talese Blackraven watched as Cammy stationed herself near the kitchen door. "Have you thought about hiding and jumping out at him?"

"Should I?" Cammy hesitated a moment, then recognized the amusement in Tally's black eyes. "Oh . . . you're kidding." Later it would probably strike her—Talese had actually made a joke! But for now she had just one thing on her mind: Ensuring that Adam's birthday supper was perfect.

"You look beautiful, missy," the housekeeper said.

A moment later Adam came in from the garage, and the expression that flickered over his face when he saw Cammy reinforced Tally's rare praise.

Cammy *felt* beautiful—freshly showered and perfumed; hair shiny clean in its bouncy new style; her soft skin glowing and delicately blushed. Deciding the occasion called for one of the gorgeous evening gowns Adam had bought her, she'd chosen to wear a pink coral silk charmeuse blouson dress, slim and sleeveless with a scoop neck and a sash at the hip. Her strappy sandals were of a deep shade of pink that complemented the dress better than a true match would have done. Luckily the single strand of pearls with ear studs that Adam had presented to her on their Dallas trip went well with the outfit.

Adam came to a rather hasty stop, his gray eyes drifting over her in a way that made Cammy's stomach quiver. She shivered, as if he were touching her.

Suddenly his lashes lowered, as though to hide the smoky emotion behind his gaze, and he said hoarsely, "Good evening, Cammy." Clearing his throat he added, "Evening, Tally. Something smells wonderful."

"You can thank your wife for that." Tally nodded at Cammy. "She's been cooking most of the afternoon."

Adam's eyes brushed her again fleetingly and then he moved over to inspect the containers atop the stove and in the oven. "Chicken à la something-or-other? Scalloped potatoes, asparagus, homemade rolls. Chocolate pie. I'm impressed."

"I was going to bake you a birthday cake, but Tally said you'd rather have the pie."

"She was right. The pie looks delicious. So does everything else. And the way you're dressed, I think I'd better change into something more appropriate." Reaching up to loosen his tie, he started toward his bedroom. "I'll be back in a few minutes."

"No, wait." Cammy caught his sleeve. "I don't want you to change—just to get comfortable. Give me your coat, and I'll get rid of it for you. Tally needs to serve the food before things get cold."

He complied, shrugging out of his jacket and watching Cammy drape it over a chair in the breakfast nook. Every step she took tonight, every gesture she made, seemed garnished with uncommon grace. Had she always moved like that—like a dancer, an angel, a walker on air? Observing the way the silk caressed her slender curves made his breath catch painfully in his chest.

She approached and slipped her hand through his arm. Her expression remained solemn for a moment, then broke up as a giggle escaped. "I was going to say something like 'You may escort me in to dinner now, Mr. Neil,' but I can't quite pull it off." Glancing down at herself she laughed again as they went into the dining room, still arm-in-arm. "I keep wondering what Gran would think if she could see me now. She'd probably scold me for putting on airs."

Adam seated her, then took the chair next to hers. "I doubt that." His voice was low, and he appeared to be too busy spreading his napkin on his lap to look at Cammy. "I imagine she would be just as dazzled as I am."

"Dazzled?" She peered at him, certain he had to be teasing. "You're dazzled by me?"

Adam was grateful that Talese brought in the first course just then, because it saved him from answering. The last thing he wanted to admit was how shattered he felt every time he looked at Cammy...how his soul felt wrenched apart with need for something more substantial than a smile.

A kiss. That would help. The memory of her lips soft and warm on his tormented him in his sleep each night. Those tender fingers stroking his cheek soothed and yet haunted his dreams....

"Adam?"

She was speaking to him, sounding perplexed, and it took him a moment to dash the cobwebs from his mind. "Yes?" he asked tersely.

"I asked how it went in court today. You pleaded a case this morning, didn't you?"

"Oh. Oh, yes! Yes, I did." And he sank back into his fog.

As the meal progressed, Cammy grew as quiet as Adam. She wanted desperately to please him, but she couldn't read his response at all. Although he complimented her on the dinner several times, he ate less than usual, which made her wonder how sincere his appreciation was. Even more worrisome was the tension vibrating the air between them; it told her he was acutely tuned in to her every move.

In turn, his awareness made *her* aware. Never had she found it so difficult to be this close to him, to endure his tantalizing scent. If she could touch him, it might have been different. But then, if she were free to touch him the way she wanted, *everything* would probably have been different, she thought with an inner sigh of hunger. This hunger was more emotional than physical. Yes, she yearned to feel his arms around her, his lips on hers, but what she desired more than anything was for Adam to care about her. Really care. Only he didn't. He was too... too isolated.

Finally they finished eating. This was the time that she usually dreaded, when Adam went off to work on something he'd brought home from the office. Once in a while he rented a movie to watch with Cammy, or at least sat in the same room with her, reading or making quiet conversation, but more often she was left to do her needlework alone in front of the television in the den.

In an attempt to postpone their parting as long as she could, Cammy stood up and smoothed the skirt of her dress. "I haven't given you your present yet."

Adam had just been thinking that he'd better end the evening, and soon. In a peculiar way it would be almost a relief to get away from her. He didn't want to dwell on the terrible letdown that it would be as well.

Rising, too, he said, "You've done more than enough already, Cammy. There was no need to buy me a gift."

She just smiled and beckoned him to follow her, and Adam went, although not without hesitation.

When he saw that she was leading him to her bedroom, his misgivings multiplied. He clenched his jaw and thrust a fist into his pocket, thinking this was likely going to prove even more of an emotional strain than dining with her had been.

Cammy opened the door and entered the room, but Adam stopped on the threshold. Inside, she stood beside the bed, her hand gesturing to the bed covering.

At first he didn't understand that she was showing him his gift, but then he realized he'd seen her piecing this particular quilt top together, and it dawned on him that she must have made it for him.

That knowledge rendered a smashing blow to the wall of detachment that usually fortified him, and his defenses started to crumble. He took a step closer, and another, and another, then just stood there, his gaze fixed downward.

The quilt was made up of an intricate series of circular designs, colorful patchwork rings interlocked with each other and appliquéd on a light blue background. There must have been a million tiny, even, handsewn stitches that followed the curving lines throughout the entire pattern, along the scalloped edges and rounded corners. The quilt reached nearly to the floor on both sides of Cammy's bed, which meant it would just fit Adam's four-poster.

The thought of how much time and work she had put into this momentarily overwhelmed him. Without raising his head he asked in a tight voice, "Is this for me?"

Cammy had never seen Adam look so shaken, unless maybe it was the night of the fire. Fighting to quell the engulfing fear that she had somehow goofed, she took a quick breath and made herself answer. "Yes, it is. Tally let me see your bedroom so I would know what colors to use. She said your mother had a double wedding ring quilt like this when she first married your father, and I thought..."

Her explanation trailed off into an uncomfortable silence. Her idea had been foolish. Adam must *hate* the quilt!

After a virtual eternity he said, "We'd better see how it looks in my room, hadn't we?"

Still unsure what his verdict was, she helped him gather up and fold the heavy blanket. He put it under one arm and indicated that she should lead the way.

Cammy had to order herself not to gawk once they reached the master bedroom, the big multiwindowed room that had originally belonged to Adam's parents. The other time she was in here, she had been tempted to stay and soak up the serene ambiance. Now the drapes were closed, shutting out the moonlit yard, but the room still beckoned, infusing her with contentment. Something about the creamy walls and carpeting with their navy blue accents made Cammy feel she had come home. And that was a risky feeling, one she'd better watch out for!

When they had spread the quilt out on his bed, he surveyed it, then smiled at her—the familiar slow half smile that had the power to tug at her heart. "It's the most beautiful gift anyone's ever given me, Cammy."

Cammy released her breath in a gasp of relief. "You like it?"

"Very much."

She tilted her head to one side. "You mean . . . you're happy with it?"

He sat down on the bed to look at her, a hand gripping the quilt on either side of him. "That's what I just said. What do I have to do to convince you?"

"You could try smiling."

"I thought I *was* smiling," he said quizzically.

"I would give a year of my life to see you smile for once like you really mean it."

The left corner of his mouth twitched. "I'm afraid this is the best I can do." After a brief hesitation he added, "Damn this face of mine! I thought you knew . . . some of the nerves were damaged, so the muscles on the left side don't respond the way I intend. I'm sorry—"

Before he could finish Cammy moved swiftly until she was standing right in front of him. Her expression infinitely tender, she covered his mouth with her hand to stop his apology, then used both palms to frame his lean cheeks.

Then, instead of rebuking him for cursing his face, she cast aside all caution and common sense and kissed him.

At first he seemed too startled to object, and then she thought he must have forgotten that he wouldn't have let her this close under ordinary circumstances. The stiffness began to drain out of his muscles, and he reached for her waist.

The next thing she knew, she was sitting on his lap, securely anchored by his strong grip, and Adam was breathing her name and kissing *her*.

A warm comforter of pleasure enveloped her as the kiss lengthened, and Cammy melted from the sweet intensity of feeling. Her arms twined around his neck, and her fingers laced urgently through his thick dark hair. After a while his mouth slid down to her throat, and she felt his hand behind her, unzipping her dress. His fingers slipped between the folds to stroke the silky skin of her back. When he pulled the bodice down off her shoulders, his hand found her bare breast and his thumb grazed the taut nipple, and at that moment, sensations began to riot inside her.

"This is ... heavenly," she gasped, aflame with joy.

Adam merely groaned and buried his face in her hair. He gathered her against him again, holding her so tightly she could barely breathe. "My Lord, but you smell good, Cammy!"

"Your heart is pounding like a jackhammer."

"I feel as if I have a finger stuck in an electrical socket."

She arched her body closer to him. "You, too?"

He groaned deeply, then growled, "Watch it, Cammy. I want you."

She repeated in an awed whisper, "You, too?"

He sat for a minute, motionless except for the spasmodic trembling that he couldn't seem to control. Then he set her aside, stood and strode to the door, which he closed. And then he switched off the light and returned to her, stripping off his shirt as he came.

Chapter Eleven

The first time they made love, Adam was driven by a wild fevered passion. He all but tore off his clothes and then hers in his desperation to quench the need that had been building inside him ever since the night he carried Cammy out of the fire.

After that initial frenzy he slowed down to savor the sweet glory, to prolong each moment even as he concentrated on pleasing her. His mouth was searching, his hands tender, his body hard and persuasive and endlessly satisfying.

When it seemed that neither had the strength to move anymore, Cammy nestled against him in the dark, her hand resting over his thudding heart. She was so blissfully tired she couldn't think straight, but then she didn't need to think to know she loved Adam Neil. This was the kind of love her grandparents had been fortunate enough to share for fifty years—the kind to die for. After what happened tonight, she thought Adam might love her, too, at least a little. If that was true, it would help ease the sorrow of her recent losses—Gran, her beloved home, her cousins.

As her fingertips traced languidly over the damp skin of his chest, his shoulders and arms, her subconscious mind noted the uneven patches amid the smooth and registered the fact that the rumors had been correct. Adam's clothes hid scars...a lot of scars. She fell asleep caressing places that had once been ravaged, shutting out of her mind unbearable thoughts of the pain he must have endured, and questions about how he had come to be trapped in the fire in the first place...a fire that killed his brother.

When she woke up the next morning, those troublesome thoughts were gone for the moment. So was Adam, but she really hadn't expected him to be there. After all, for perhaps the second time in her life she had slept past ten o'clock, and he always left for work by eight-thirty.

Feeling lazy, a little smug, and very, very lucky, Cammy lay for a while snuggled under the quilt she had given him. With Adam's lingering scent in the bed evoking delicious memories of the night before, she enjoyed a daydream about what would happen tonight.

When she finally made it to the kitchen, she realized that Talese knew exactly what had happened. The quiet woman seemed aware of *everything* that went on in the house.

"Tally," Cammy said hesitantly as she sat drinking coffee at the table while the housekeeper shelled peas, "I've been meaning to ask you something for a while now...."

Tally grunted, a vaguely encouraging sound.

"You've known Adam since he was little, haven't you?"

Tally's look narrowed to suspicion and she shrugged.

"Could you please tell me what he was like back then?"

"I am not good at describing." She cleared her throat. "Maybe you should ask Adam."

"Are you joking? He won't talk about himself." Frustrated, she added, "I just thought you could help me know him better. Even though we've been neighbors forever, he's eleven years older than me. He was almost grown by the time I really remember seeing him. I just wondered what he looked like as a child...what he liked to do, how he had fun...that sort of thing."

"Adam has no great affection for the past."

"I know." She smiled apologetically. "That's why I asked you."

Tally didn't respond for so long, Cammy began to think she wasn't going to. Then finally she stood and wiped her hands on a kitchen towel. "Come with me."

She led Cammy to another of the spare bedrooms in the sprawling house and opened a polished cedar chest at the foot of the bed. The odor of mothballs assailed them as Tally removed a crocheted bedspread ivoried with age. Underneath were several boxes, some holding bundles of letters tied together with ribbon, others containing hundreds of old photographs.

Tally lifted out the boxes of snapshots and put them on the bed. "There," she muttered. "Now you can see how he looked, before."

While Cammy was still protesting that Tally had misread her intentions, the housekeeper departed, and she was left alone with her curiosity and a very big temptation.

Adam took two aspirins just before he left the office for home. His head ached, partly because he hadn't gotten enough sleep last night, and partly as a result of subsequent events of the day.

Sometime before daybreak that morning, the exquisite fulfillment he felt with Cammy had changed to guilt and shame when he started to consider what he had done. "You'll be safe here," he'd promised her before their marriage. "You won't have to sleep with me. I'll never make any unwanted advances."

The least he could have done was keep that promise, no matter how hard it was...and in the past few weeks it had grown nearly impossible. His willpower had weakened day by day, and her unbelievable generosity the night before had finally broken him. For his birthday gift, he had taken not just the quilt, but her innocence!

You should have tried harder to keep away, he railed at himself as he drove, vowing never to betray her trust like that again.

He dreaded the thought of facing her. Somehow he had to figure out a way to hide his obsession with her...to keep her from learning that he dreamed about her both waking and sleeping. That he wanted to move her permanently into his bedroom, into his life, and never let her go.

She was already woven into the very fabric of his heart, and it was up to him to tear her out of it. She felt nothing for him. Nothing but gratitude, perhaps, and after last night, pity. He'd felt her fingertips on his body, exploring the scars that had been too extensive to be helped by plastic surgery.

Lance had warned Cammy not to marry him for the wrong reasons, and she had said...what? To the best of his memory, she hadn't denied feeling either gratitude or pity.

Adam rubbed distractedly at his throbbing temples, thinking of Cammy's cousin. That morning he had run into Lance in the lobby of the courthouse, where another heated confrontation ensued. Lance must have finally seen

the light and realized it would cost him more than it was
worth to sue Cammy, with very little hope of winning.
Angry over that, he'd tried to intimidate Adam into making Ted Nix move his cattle off the Anderson farm. When
that failed, he began snarling insults at Adam, dragging up
all the old talk about Colby, twisting the truth beyond
recognition. The whole scene had been loud and embar-
rassing, even though Adam had mostly just listened and
shook his head, and finally walked away in disgust.

He would do anything to get that creep off Cammy's
case once and for all. Anything except advise her to sell the
farm. Let the greedy vulture suffer for the way he'd been
acting. Adam ignored the voice in his head that pointed
out he was getting remarkably little satisfaction out of
punishing Lance.

At home, he had to steel himself to enter the kitchen.
When he did, it was every bit as bad as he'd expected.
Cammy was helping Tally fix supper, and when he came
in, she turned and smiled at him warmly.

Confused by the fierce rush of love he felt, Adam
wanted to open his arms and wrap himself around her, but
he reminded himself that last night had been the biggest
mistake of his life. The only thing he'd done right was to
turn off the light, and even that hadn't helped much. With
those gentle fingers of hers, Cammy had still managed to
discover all his scars. That was what her tender smile now
was about—she felt sorry for any poor soul trapped in a
body that looked like his.

His sudden anger was directed as much to himself as to
his wife. He nodded curtly to her, spoke to Tally, and
strode on to his bedroom without stopping.

Cammy felt as if he had jerked the rug out from under
her and sent her sprawling. Her welcoming smile vanished

as she glanced at Talese. "I guess he had a bad day." Tally just stared after him.

Supper was a disaster. Cammy tried at first to make pleasant conversation, but after a while, when Adam barely acknowledged her comments, she lapsed into silence. She had no idea what she had done to displease him. She had thought last night would have changed things.

It changed things, all right, she told herself sadly. Always before he'd been polite. Now he ignored her.

Maybe it was her performance he didn't like. A hot flush stained Cammy's cheeks as the idea took hold. That was probably it. She didn't have enough experience to please him. And there wasn't a heck of a lot she could do to remedy that, without his cooperation.

By the time they'd finished eating, she only wanted to escape his cool presence, his aloof gray eyes. She mumbled good-night and went straight to bed, forgetting to help Talese, deciding not to work on the new quilt she'd started, just showering and crawling as quickly as possible between the sheets. Gamely she put her humiliation out of her mind.

It occurred to her just before she drifted off that there seemed to be a lot of unsafe topics for thought lately.

Adam tried to sleep, but instead he tossed and turned, unable to think about anything except Cammy. Her sunny optimism and kind heart. Her slim body curled up against him. Her alluring scent. The magic touch of her fingers. Her silky lips nuzzling him just where it felt best....

The confusion and pain in her wide blue eyes at the way he talked to her, or rather *didn't* talk to her, tonight.

He flopped over onto his back, flung an arm across his forehead, and swore at himself. His callous behavior had been uncalled for. Cammy might not love him, but she had liked and respected him, even after last night. But now? The way she had left the dining room as if the devil were on her heels made him wonder just how badly he had hurt her.

His jaws clenched, he sat up and stared through the darkness at nothing. What did he plan to do about it? He couldn't apologize without explaining why he'd acted like such a bastard. And there was no way he could explain.

Sighing, he got out of bed, felt around for the brown robe that he'd draped over one bedpost, and thrust his arms into the sleeves. He wouldn't get any sleep tonight if he didn't at least check on Cammy, make sure she was okay.

He opened her door very quietly. There was an eerie glow in the room that startled him at first, until he saw that it streamed through her windows where she'd thrown open the curtains so she could see the stars. Cammy lay in a pool of glistening moonlight on the bed, her hair fanned out in a dark tangle on the pillow.

Adam stepped into the room before he realized what he was going to do, and once inside, he shut the door silently behind him. That slender, still figure drew him as compellingly as if she were reeling him in on a line. He stood there a moment, gazing down at her, at the white silk nightgown outlining her shape, and a well of love and need bubbled up in him. He wanted her now as badly as he had wanted her last night. The heat in his bloodstream was suddenly just as potent, just as nearly out of control.

Adam's palms grew damp, and he knotted his hands into fists. *Stop this!* he ordered himself silently, his forehead beading with perspiration and his throat constricting. *Leave her. It's not meant to be.*

But he couldn't make himself go. His eyes devoured her in the ethereal light, his heart thudding much too fast for either his health or his peace of mind, and while he stood there frozen in anguish, she stirred and opened her eyes.

He jerked back. Too late. She sat up, blinking, "Adam?"

His mouth was dry, his heart in his throat. He wanted to say something casual, something to reassure her, but all he could do was whisper in strangled tones, "Oh, Lord, Cammy... what am I doing here?"

Her bewildered eyes searched his. "Sleepwalking?"

He tried to smile but knew from the way it felt that the result was even more twisted than usual. "I wish I could claim that excuse." His voice was low, taut. "I came to see you...to tell you..." Groaning, he pivoted and plowed his fingers through his hair, his distress so intense he couldn't hide it.

"What?" she asked softly. No matter how much he had hurt her earlier, she could never want to hurt him back. "Tell me what?"

Turning, he sank down onto the bed and reached for her hand, then sheathed it tightly between both of his. She squeezed back, a sign that she was listening, and just that little bit of contact sent a jolting shock through him. He promptly forgot everything except his aching need for Cammy.

Within seconds she was in his arms, pulled close against his chest. His lips were on her eyes, her ears, her throat. "I can't stay away," he murmured huskily. "I tried, but I can't."

Cammy didn't understand it—she just accepted it. "Nobody said you had to stay away, Adam."

She drew back a little, far enough to slip one hand between them and untie the belt of his robe. Then she tugged it off his hard, square shoulders and started undoing the tiny pearl buttons down the front of her gown.

He helped her, and soon they lay together, limbs entwined, male angles and female curves molding skin against skin into one being with two furiously pounding hearts. For a long breathless interlude, passion prevailed. Gradually it gave way to shuddering contentment, and finally, sleep.

Night eased into that time just before daybreak when things seem blackest. Waking with a start, Adam ran his fumbling hand down the smooth length of Cammy's thigh and realized with a sinking feeling just where he was. He'd done it again. Dismayed with his weakness, he eased out from beneath her arm.

Cammy got used to Adam's peculiar mood swings. Actually they began to conform to a fairly predictable pattern. Every day he acted cool, remote, businesslike. Never rude; just not very...accessible. No friendly give and take. No touching. Sort of a lawyer-client relationship, where the lawyer and client in question happen to share the same house.

And then, almost every night, he shared her bed. He never started out there, and she was pretty sure he didn't intend to end up there either, but sometime after midnight he would slip into her room. She began staying awake, waiting for him, praying he would come. When he did, they would make love, cuddle, make love some more, and finally doze off, until sometime before dawn, when Adam would quietly take himself off. Regularly, like clockwork.

And then, the next day, more of his brooding reserve.

Why he behaved like that was beyond her comprehension. She unhappily concluded that she had been wrong about his loving her. He couldn't care very much or he wouldn't treat her with such disinterest most of the time.

There were plenty of things she didn't understand about Adam, she realized, but that didn't make her love him any less. Hoping for answers, she returned to the boxes of pictures, and that evening she even went so far as to tell him she'd been looking through them.

Her news jarred him out of his detachment. He lifted his head sharply, his fork poised in midair. "Why?"

"I just wanted to learn more about your family."

"My family." He put down the fork, grimacing. "And what did you learn from the pictures?"

"I learned—" She stopped uncertainly. It probably wasn't a good idea to tell him how she'd felt studying photographs of him before he was burned. She couldn't find the words to say that even as a little boy, his eyes had been grave and intelligent and capable of making her heart slide into a melting tailspin... that his mobile, expressive, untwisted mouth had been more sensitive than she would ever have believed... that his face had been lean and beautifully sculpted, with a bone structure that could never be ruined by surface scars.

No, she didn't think she could tell him that. Nor could she say his brother Colby had struck her as a poor imitation of Adam—not so tall, not so well-built, not anywhere near so handsome, with his habitual sneering grin.

"I saw your father," she blurted instead. "I didn't remember him at all."

Something flickered in his eyes. "You must have been very small when he died. I was fourteen."

Gently, she asked, "Did he have a heart attack?"

He nodded. "He was only in his forties. At the time I thought he'd been cheated. Later I realized how lucky he was."

"Lucky?"

"He died quickly, before all hell broke loose. Before this." He indicated his face with one hand. "It took my mother years to die from a broken heart."

Appalled, Cammy could only stammer, "Your mother...I loved her. She was so...so lovely and sweet. I never...she didn't act as if she had a broken heart."

"My mother was a Southern gentlewoman. She kept her troubles to herself." Then his face softened. "She loved you, too," he said unexpectedly, almost roughly. "You and Miss Louella. There was one particularly low moment in her life when your grandmother kept her from giving up." He fiddled aimlessly with his napkin, his eyes averted. "A time when I wasn't much help to her."

Something told her that he was talking about the time following the fire. How Gran had helped, she couldn't imagine, and she didn't dare ask.

"I think," he mused slowly, "Mother would like you to have her jewelry. One of these days I'll get the best pieces out of the safe-deposit box. In the meantime Tally can show you where the rest is kept here at home."

When Cammy tried to protest that she couldn't possibly take anything so valuable, Adam assumed a bitter look. "Just what am I supposed to do with it? You're my wife—the only one I have. Who do you suggest I give it to?"

As gracefully as possible she gave in. "Well, then...I'd be proud to wear your mother's jewelry, Adam, just as I'm proud to be part of the Neil family."

He actually laughed at that—not a humorous sound. "I haven't taught you very much about family yet, have I? Dig a little deeper into the history of this generation of Neils, my love, and I guarantee you'll be cured of your idealism once and for all."

His "my love" was sardonic, cutting, definitely not to be mistaken for an endearment.

As if to underscore that, he didn't come to Cammy later that night, which gave her something else to think about. And for once she quit denying and *thought*.

After a miserable night, Cammy hoped a good talk with Margo would help set her mind straight, although she wasn't sure she could bring herself to be honest. But she had to try. A quick phone call after breakfast confirmed that Margo could meet her for lunch.

"Would you drop off some things at the cleaners while you are in town?" Tally asked.

Cammy agreed and accompanied the housekeeper to Adam's bedroom. Tally removed an armload of suits from the closet and laid them on the bed, and then she and Cammy went through the pockets. Tally had advised her of the danger of misplacing a scrap of paper bearing important information Adam might have scribbled down in court.

Instead of Adam's notes to himself, Cammy discovered a jewelry box in one coat pocket. Puzzled, she opened it and found a rich-looking ring inside—a man's ring.

Funny, Adam had told her when they bought her simple gold wedding band that he never wore rings.

"I wonder what this is doing here." She displayed the box for Tally. When the woman merely frowned and shrugged, Cammy slipped the ring out of its velvet setting and held it up to the light. Inside the band she found the engraved inscription, *"Love, April."*

Love, April? Dear God! Cammy felt so sick that she was suddenly afraid she would pass out cold on the floor. She looked up speechlessly at Tally, who grabbed her arm and made her sit down on the bed. "What's the matter, missy?"

Several minutes passed before Cammy could manage a response, and then she had to swallow hard first. "I guess I should have paid more attention to my grandmother. She always told me snoopers never learn good news."

"Let me see that." When Tally had read the message, a grim look came over her face. She jammed the ring back into its slot, then snapped the box shut and slapped it down on the dresser. "That woman! Has she not done enough? You should not—no, you *must not* think this means anything."

Cammy knew Talese would never believe Adam capable of any immorality. As for her, she wasn't sure what she believed. The ring was pretty damaging evidence.

Somehow she manufactured a smile and stood. "Let's finish and put these clothes in my car."

"You still going to town?" Tally inquired anxiously.

"Why not?" After all, life had to go on, even when the heartache reached overwhelming proportions.

Chapter Twelve

"**E**xactly what is it that's bugging you, Cam?" Margo persisted after nearly an hour of not-so-subtle prying. The two were eating hamburgers in Cammy's car beneath the awning at the Sonic drive-in, able to bear the August heat only because the car top was down and a pleasant breeze was drifting through town.

Shrugging in response to Margo's question, Cammy hunched down in the seat and adjusted the brim of her floppy straw hat a bit lower as if to shade her eyes from the sun. Actually it was a disguise. Not that anyone could fail to recognize the car Adam Neil had bought for his wife. One thing about red convertibles, they attracted plenty of attention.

"Tell me what's wrong," Margo said with relentless patience. "You know I won't give up until you do."

Cammy avoided her friend's eyes, studying her own interlaced fingers as she said very quietly, "Remember when you warned me about April Magness?"

"Is *that* it?" Margo's face grew thoughtful as she shook her head. "But why now? She seems to have given up on Adam. I haven't seen her go into his office in weeks."

All that meant, Cammy thought with an uncharacteristic spurt of cynicism, was that April and Adam were becoming sneakier.

"Anyway, you have no reason to worry about April. The woman's not exactly known for her wit and intelligence. And heck, Camelia, you're way ahead of her when it comes to looks. In fact, you're about the closest thing Comanche has to a fashion model, what with your new haircut and all those classy clothes." Margo eyed her long and hard. "You really have changed, and I'm not just talking about the way you dress. You look like you know what you want out of life. I guess we can thank Adam for that." She wiggled her eyebrows, then frowned. "You seem so sure of yourself these days, I sometimes get the feeling I don't know you anymore."

Margo's observation was right, at least in part—Cammy finally knew what she wanted out of life. She wanted Adam, forever. But the only thing she was sure of was that her chances of getting what she wanted were slim.

By the time Adam got home from work that evening, Cammy had concluded that she was going to have to pursue several matters with him, despite his reticence. During supper she never quite came up with the right opening, and the moment he finished eating he glanced at his wristwatch and excused himself, saying he had to meet a client in town.

Sure, you do, she thought, annoyed. *A client named April?* She followed him to the garage and called his name just as he started to get into his car. Turning, he stood with his hand on the door as she approached. "Today I heard that the nursing home needs someone to run the kitchen."

He lifted one shoulder and dropped it. "So?"

She was facing him now with the open car door between them. "That's a job I could handle."

Raising an eyebrow, he looked down at her disdainfully. "I'm sure there are plenty of jobs you could handle, Cammy. Whether you would enjoy doing them the rest of your life is another question."

"I can think of worse things than cooking for old folks." She tilted up her chin. "Besides, beggars can't be choosers."

"You're not a beggar," he said, his voice sharp.

"I'm certainly not independent," she argued and decided to try another tack. "A woman in Margo's office was telling me that a new training class for nurses begins next month in Stephenville. I'm thinking of driving over there tomorrow to check on it."

Looking eager to finish this conversation, Adam drummed the fingers of one hand on the window. "If you really want to be a nurse, I'd recommend that you look into an RN program. One that will provide you with a Bachelor of Science degree."

Her mouth fell open. Here she was trying to find the quickest way to let him off the hook, and he was suggesting that she commit herself to a four-year endeavor! "I hope you're kidding. I'd be in school until I'm an old lady!"

The right side of his mouth twitched, as if he were trying hard not to smile, and she suddenly itched to slap the mocking amusement from his face, especially when he said, "Mmm-hmm. An old lady of twenty-five." His gray eyes narrowed as if something had just occurred to him, and he abruptly slammed the door shut and propped one lean hip against it, crossing his arms on his chest. "Is there some pressing reason you can't go to college?"

"Isn't it obvious?" she snapped. "I need to get a job so I can support myself."

A trace of something more complex than mere impatience shaded his dark features. "Don't be ridiculous. You're not desperate. That's why you married me, remember? You can take your time and find a career you'll really like."

Her blue eyes glittering, she went up on her tiptoes to get closer to his face—that half-flawed face she found herself wanting, even now, in the midst of her anger, to cover with soft kisses. "I haven't forgotten why I married you, Adam. Not for a minute. But maybe you'd care to tell me how I can ever hope to find a career when you tear apart every single idea I come up with?"

Then, a little shocked at herself, she took a step back. For the first time in her life she had spoken sarcastically to him, and there was plenty more she wanted to say. It took all her willpower not to throw herself at him, to beat his chest with her fists in hurt fury. She didn't want to share him with April Magness!

A guarded look settling over his face, he uncrossed his arms and pushed his hands deep into his pockets. "I don't mean to tear your ideas apart. It's just that...you seem so well suited to what you do around here—baking, gardening, making quilts—that I thought you enjoyed it. I thought you were happy..." His voice trailed off, and an unusual flush crept up his cheeks. For a moment he stared down at his shoes, almost as if he were embarrassed, scuffing one polished toe across a stain on the cement garage floor, then lifted his eyes to meet hers again with reluctance. "I'm sorry. By all means, look into any training program that interests you. I'm sure you know better than I what you want to do with the rest of your life."

I want to spend my life taking care of you, she thought
ut didn't dare admit it, knowing what she did about
April.

Adam had offered to meet his client at his office after
iours because the woman, who was trying to regain cus-
ody of her children after a messy divorce, couldn't get
ime off from her job. He didn't get home until almost ten
'clock, and he was puzzled to find the red convertible
;one when he pulled into the garage.

"Where's Cammy?" he asked Tally, who was prepar-
ng to soak a big pot of red beans overnight.

"She went for a drive. She said not to wait up."

He didn't like that at all. The truth was, he had been
preoccupied ever since their talk earlier—anxious for
nidnight to come so he could try to heal their relation-
hip. Every night that he stayed away from her, as he had
lone the night before, seemed to stretch into an eternity of
oneliness. "She has no business going out alone at night,"
ie grumbled. "Couldn't you have stopped her?"

Tally gave him an odd look, which was really all his
question deserved.

"Sorry," he muttered after a moment. He sighed deeply,
an a tired hand down his face, and started to go to his
oom, then remembered the request he'd made of Tally
hat morning. "Did you give Cammy my mother's jew-
·lry?"

"I will do that tomorrow." She pursed her lips as she
washed her hands and picked up something from the cab-
net. "I got sidetracked this morning getting your clothes
eady for the cleaners. This was in one of your pockets."

He took the box, then frowned. April's ring! He'd for-
;otten it completely. "April Magness gave this to me," he
aid. "A birthday present."

Tally grunted. "Seems to me you got a lot of birthday presents this year...some more valuable than others. Did you have trouble deciding which you should keep?"

Although he wasn't sure what she was getting at, he had a sinking sense of foreboding. "Did Cammy see this?"

Tally's look of reproof told him she had.

Well, he thought dispiritedly as he got ready for bed, maybe he should just let Cammy believe whatever she liked about April. It might be the most effective way to prevent her from guessing that he'd fallen foolishly, incautiously, hopelessly in love with her. It was becoming clear to him that Cammy wanted out of the marriage. Every day she seemed stronger, more capable of standing up for herself.

And he wanted that for her, he assured himself after searching his heart with painful honesty. He just didn't know how he was going to stand it when she left him.

Cammy and Adam avoided each other as much as possible for a miserable week, except for a couple of midnight visits that Adam simply didn't have the strength to stop himself from making. Those stolen hours were all that kept him going, in fact. If he hadn't been able to lose himself in her sunshine fragrance and her warm whispered gentleness, he probably would have paid with his sanity. Dear Lord, if only he could have more of her than just the darkest part of the night!

Their few daytime encounters were awkward and tense, especially the time Cammy broached the possibility of putting Gran's farm on the market now that Ted Nix had sold most of his herd and moved the rest onto Neil land. Lately she had been swamped with a sense of being abandoned...so abandoned that she'd entertained desperate thoughts of making amends with her cousins. Selling the farm was the only way she knew to accomplish that.

Once more Adam curtly made it clear that he advised against selling, confounding her with legal jargon that she suspected was nothing but fancy double-talk. What it boiled down to, she figured, was that he hated her family and would do anything to thwart their wishes, secure in the knowledge that she owed him too much to disagree.

Why? she asked herself with frustration. Was it really something about the Andersons or maybe just families in general that he scorned? Or was it the Neils?

Dig much deeper into the Neil family history and you'll be cured of your idealism, Adam had taunted her.

Had that been a veiled challenge? If so, Cammy knew where to dig. The cedar chest in the spare bedroom held plenty of memorabilia besides just photos. While Talese poked through boxes and removed the lovely pieces of turquoise and silver jewelry that Adam wanted her to have, Cammy sat on the bed, running a hand over the letters bound in ribbon. She discovered most of them had been addressed in a dear, familiar handwriting to Joanne Neil care of the burn treatment center of a major medical center in Galveston.

"These are from Gran," she murmured when Tally had finished. The housekeeper nodded silently. Cammy's teeth caught her bottom lip and tugged at it. "I suppose you know what's in them?"

"I can guess. It was a very bad time."

By now Cammy knew that Tally's gruffness covered feelings too deep for words. She looked at the older woman with pleading, hopeful eyes. "Could you tell me about that time?"

Tally just shook her head as if it were beyond her.

"Please, Tally! If only I knew for sure why Adam has so much hate inside him, maybe I could help."

"It is not hate that is a slow poison in his heart," Tally said fiercely. "It is hurt. That much I can tell you. As for the rest—" her dark eyes slid to the letters and then back to meet Cammy's "—you must figure that out yourself." And she turned and left the room, pulling the door shut behind her.

Cammy sat without moving for a long time, the tip of her index finger just touching the old-fashioned script on the first envelope. She ached inside with a poignant need for her grandmother and her special brand of wisdom.

After a while, drawing an unsteady breath, she lifted the flap and removed the folded sheets of paper, then opened them and began to read.

Hours later Tally returned and found Cammy curled up on the bed, red-eyed and sniffly. She stopped in the doorway, her stern face lined with worry. "You okay, miss?"

Cammy sat up sluggishly and nodded. Her head throbbed and her heart felt all wrung out with anguish. From little things Louella Anderson had written to Mrs. Neil in a series of letters over a year-and-a-half span while Adam underwent medical treatment, Cammy had pieced together a picture of two brothers, the older one quiet, intelligent, having an innate sense of pride and honor, the joy and hope of his father and mother. Less was said about the younger, who was dead by that time; but still there emerged a portrait of a youth with an inherently flawed personality—self-centered, vain, and filled with a greed that far exceeded his years, someone who constantly made demands and stirred up trouble, both within his family and without.

She could only imagine the agony Colby Neil had dragged his parents through before he died, and the efforts they had made to treat both boys the same. But instilling a love of family evidently hadn't been possible with

Colby, who had grown to despise his brother and the admiration Adam seemed to earn so easily.

After Mr. Neil's sudden death, Colby must have started thinking ahead to his own eventual inheritance, and he apparently began plotting ways to avoid sharing any of the Neil wealth with Adam. Adam had known only that Colby was jealous of him, that he tried his best to sabotage Adam's interests, that he'd even taken Adam's first car without asking and wrecked it. Colby's resentment had escalated, while Adam, out of blind loyalty, still hadn't realized the extent of his brother's irrational hatred.

And then something had happened concerning an unnamed girl. *April,* Cammy deduced glumly. She had supposedly been Colby's girlfriend but had begun flirting with Adam, and that must have sent Colby over the edge. Although the details weren't spelled out, it was clear from Gran's mention of the investigation that Colby had laid a trap for Adam in the old barn, intending to burn it down over his head and kill him. But Colby had died instead, evidently kicked in the head by one of the fear-crazed horses, and Adam had survived, so hurt in body and spirit at the age of seventeen that for a time he didn't even seem to want to live. More devastating than the burns was the knowledge of what his brother had tried to do to him.

Gran had written Joanne Neil often, bolstering her faith, imploring her to remember Adam's former strength of body and character and treat him as if he were the same. Reminding her that she must not give in to despair—not if she expected Adam to make it.

And there, mixed in with those letters, were some Gran had written to Adam during that same period . . . warm, loving notes in which she encouraged him to weather the storm for his mother's sake. *If you give up, Adam dear, it will kill her. You have the determination of the Neils, that*

*wonderful inner spirit and courage. I know you can pull
through this and grow to be the sort of fine man your father was. You can be anything you want to be....*

Gran had cheered up both mother and son during their
ordeal at the distant hospital, from initial skin grafts
through later plastic surgery to repair the damage to the
most visible part of him, his face, neck, and hands. When
he decided against further surgery, she had adjured him to
trust that he had more to offer people than just a perfect
body. *Someday a woman will fall in love with you...one
who will see nothing but beauty and honor when she looks
at you...*

Boy, Gran had hit the nail on the head with that one!

While Tally watched, Cammy folded and replaced all the
letters, then tied them back up with their ribbon. When
Cammy had closed the cedar chest, she turned and reached
out, blinded by fresh tears, to cling to the taciturn woman.
Tally rocked her gently, not speaking.

Thursday evening Tally handed Adam the telephone the
minute he walked in the door. It was Freeman Burke, in-
viting Katie and himself to spend the weekend in
Comanche with Adam and Cammy. The conversation
took all of forty-five seconds. "We'll see you tomorrow
about six o'clock," Freeman said, then hung up without
giving Adam a chance to make up an excuse.

"I'll call him back and tell him not to come," Adam
muttered during supper, stewing over the proposed visit.

"You certainly will not," Cammy objected. What would
Gran say to such a lack of hospitality? What would
Adam's mother have said? "We have plenty of guest
rooms. I'll get one of them ready."

"That's not the point. Where does Freeman get off,
calling me up and announcing that he's coming?"

"He's probably worried. You said you used to drive to Dallas to see them every week or two. When was the last time you even called him?"

Adam shrugged. He had too much on his mind to think about such trivial details as chatting with his best friend. "This isn't a good time for them to visit."

"Well," Cammy said with a stubbornness she'd only recently realized she had inherited from somewhere, "I *want* them to come. We've been married two months; it's about time we had the Burkes to visit. You can do what you like, but I'm going to make them welcome."

Subsiding into grim, unsmiling thought, Adam searched out and faced the real reason behind his reluctance to entertain Freeman and Katie: his everlasting pride. He didn't want them to know Cammy didn't share his bedroom.

Well, there was one way to keep them from finding out!

"Fine," he said, pushing back from the table and standing up. "Why don't you give them *your* room? You aren't going to be needing it."

Having no idea what he was raving about, Cammy jumped up and followed him to her bedroom, where he began gathering up armloads of her clothes and personal items and carrying them down the hall to the master suite. He ignored her stammered questions until he had transferred everything onto the bed in his own room, and then he faced her and crossed his arms. "Okay, let them come. Now they'll find just what they expected—a couple of lovebirds. And don't complain, Cammy. Remember, you're the one who wanted company."

The weekend, and the Burkes, came and went. Cammy's things remained in Adam's bedroom, and Cammy never had the slightest inclination to complain. She adored the intimacy of sharing his living space, even though she wondered if he had moved her in as some kind of punishment. She was half afraid he planned to send her back to her old room, but as the days passed he never mentioned her moving. He even went to church with her again occasionally, something he'd stopped doing in the past weeks.

Cammy knew enough to keep her mouth shut. Putting school, Gran's farm, and April Magness out of her mind, she just relaxed and enjoyed the nighttimes, the pleasure of going to sleep in her husband's bed and knowing that once the lights were out he would join her—earlier and earlier, as a matter of fact. And he began staying later and later.

One morning the sun woke Cammy, and she discovered Adam still asleep beside her. Always before he'd been careful to be up and dressed before dawn, to avoid letting Cammy see the body that had worked such magic on her earlier. But evidently his mental alarm had failed to rouse him for once, and he lay sprawled on his back with a pillow covering most of his face.

Although it was her first full-daylight view of him, she wasn't shocked; her hands had already grown well acquainted with the scars, and now her eyes traced slowly and lovingly along his lean muscled torso and limbs. She could understand why he had refused to endure any more of the painful, immobilizing plastic surgery. What did the scars matter, anyway? They didn't change his essence.

Cammy was considering whether she could get away with touching him, when suddenly she felt the familiar beginnings of churning nausea. Knowing that seconds counted at a time like this, she lunged off the bed and dashed for the bathroom, where she was violently sick.

She had rinsed out her mouth and was washing her ashen face when Adam's image appeared in the mirror. He stood behind her in the doorway, knotting the belt of his

robe, and he wore a peculiar, tight-lipped look that she
didn't comprehend until he spoke. "I guess some things
are too gruesome even for my saintly wife to stomach in
the light of day," he said with bitter irony.

"Don't say that," she protested weakly, about to tell
him that she must have caught some crazy kind of virus
because she'd been nauseated nearly every morning this
week.

But Adam was turning, saying coldly over his shoulder,
"I apologize for oversleeping. To make sure it doesn't
happen again, I'll have Tally move your things back to
your own room."

Chapter Thirteen

Talese put the plate of saltine crackers and cup of hot tea on the table beside Cammy's bed. "How long will you wait before you tell Adam what is going on?"

Reaching for a cracker without sitting up, Cammy nibbled the corner off. "It's just a bug. I'll surely get over it in a day or so."

"A bug?" Tally shook her head. "You cannot really think this is a bug that makes you sick every morning for three weeks!" She eyed the young woman shrewdly. "Is your time of the month late?"

Cammy lay there with a stricken look on her face, no longer able to deny the growing fears inside her. Slowly she nodded, her eyes filled with tears that scalded as they ran down her cheeks. "What am I going to do, Tally?" she whispered. "Adam will be furious!"

"That baby is his, is it not?"

"Of course!"

"Then why should he be angry?"

"He doesn't want children."

Tally chuckled. "He may not be *anticipating* any at the moment, but that does not mean he will not be glad."

"Oh..." Cammy moaned and turned onto her side, curling up into a ball and hugging the pillow to her rebellious stomach. "You just don't know!"

"No, I do not know," the other woman agreed. "Neither do you. You must tell him soon and see if he is glad."

"I can't tell him yet!" Cammy looked at her beseechingly. "I'm not even sure I'm pregnant. You won't say a word to him until I'm ready, will you?"

"Will you see a doctor?"

"I guess I have to." Cammy glanced at the clock and ran a shaky hand through her tangled hair. She felt like something the dog dragged up and the cat wouldn't eat. "I'll try to get an appointment this morning."

"Then let us wait and see. There may be nothing to get stirred up about."

Dear Lord, let that be the case! Let it just be my hormones out of kilter! she prayed as she got dressed and headed for Stephenville. She had opted against seeing her local physician, afraid that if she were pregnant word would spread all over town before she could figure out what to do.

Two hours later she sat in the convertible beneath a shade tree at a roadside park, staring at the highway as she tried to sort out her jumbled, spinning thoughts. It was a sunny September afternoon, but she was too distracted to enjoy the cloudless blue sky or the warmth. Dr. Thompson's verdict had been definite: Cammy was pregnant. The baby would probably come late next spring.

The knowledge of the new life budding inside her awed Cammy. This was a part of Adam. This baby would give her a chance to pour out her abundant love onto a human recipient. The baby would *need* her love . . .

Unlike its father, she thought with heart-wrenching despair. He had made it plain that their marriage was a simple matter of obligation on his part, of repaying a debt to Louella Anderson. Not once had he pretended to love Cammy, nor to have any use for her affection. From the very start he had warned her he didn't want children, and she knew very well how he felt about the whole concept of family. Small wonder, considering the deep scars his brother had branded him with, both inside and out.

And as for her own family . . . well, the Andersons weren't much better. They were greedy, disloyal, hungry for spite.

So basically, there would be no family and not much of a home life for this tiny precious new being. It would do little good to remind Adam that he should have thought of birth control. He didn't seem to have much to say to Cammy these days, and he hadn't touched her since she'd moved back to her old bedroom, two weeks earlier. For all she knew, he might be spending his nights with April.

Is this what you want for your baby? she asked herself in horror, remembering the love that had surrounded her as she grew up. *And what have you done to change things for the better, Camelia? Would it kill you to sell the farm?*

Up to now she had let Adam's stubborn determination override her wishes to make peace, but she was starting to realize she couldn't afford to be her husband's puppet any longer. Adam might feel a strong urge to punish her cousins, and she could understand why. She *did* understand, and she ached for him, for his bitterness. But she had to forgive, to work harder than she'd ever worked to mend the broken boughs of her family tree. Otherwise, this baby would have nothing of any value, no matter how much wealth it might stand to inherit from its very reluctant father.

"Sam Dillby in Stephenville for you, Adam," Maggie called. "Line one."

Without adjusting his reclining position in the comfortable leather desk chair, Adam glanced at the wall clock and saw that it was almost twelve o'clock. He reached for the telephone and propped the receiver against one ear. "Hello, Sam. What's up?"

"Not much, Adam. I'm just trying to locate your wife. Thought maybe you could give me another number for her."

"Cammy?" He rubbed his eyes, then his temples, trying to fend off the tension that was slowly but surely sinking its talons into his nerves. That's what came from burying himself beneath a mountain of work. He could avoid thinking about his personal life, all right, but by noon he was a zombie. "Isn't she at home?"

"Nobody answers there."

Adam frowned as a sudden thought clicked into place. If his brain hadn't been lagging two steps behind his mouth, he would have asked this first. "Why are you looking for Cammy, anyway?"

"I wanted to let her know the papers are ready for her to sign. But there's no hurry."

"Papers?" Adam croaked in shock, sitting up so fast that he dropped the telephone. He grabbed it and stuck it back to his ear. "What papers?" he demanded hoarsely. Was Cammy planning to file for a divorce?

"Why, the papers for the sale of the Anderson farm." Mr. Dillby sounded surprised and rather hesitant. "I thought you knew about that. Otherwise I never would have called you—"

"Oh, *that*." Adam forced himself to speak nonchalantly, although he was beginning to seethe now that he was sure this wasn't a divorce they were discussing. "My mind was on something else, Sam."

"I see. Well, would you like to tell Cammy to drop by my office, or should I try her again?"

"Maybe you'd better keep trying. I won't be home until late." *If it all,* he thought with a sudden sense of futility as he hung up. Why bother pretending there was any kind of relationship remaining between Cammy and him? She was selling the farm, and she hadn't even told him. What else was she hiding from him? A secret career?

With a faint twinge of guilt he recalled that evening several weeks ago when she had confronted him and asked him—all right, *begged* him—to reconsider and help her sell the place. At the time he had thought how distraught she looked, but he hadn't let that sway him. Instead, he had pictured the cruel sneer on Lance's face when he accused Adam of killing Colby...heard again the mockery in Babette's voice as she called him a monster. And he had refused to bend an inch. So Cammy had gone behind his back.

Spurred by anger, Adam plunged into the stack of paperwork on his desk. When Maggie left at five o'clock, he told himself he really wouldn't go home that night. He would sleep on the sofa here in his office. And he did hold out until seven. But then, moving slowly, like a robot, he locked up and drove home, knowing he couldn't sleep until he knew whether Cammy would tell him the truth.

Tally was surprised to see him. Cammy, it seemed, had already eaten and was working on a quilt.

Adam startled his housekeeper even more by saying he would eat in the den with Cammy. He took his tray in and sat down nearby, greeting her with what he thought was admirable composure. "How did your day go?" he asked.

Not meeting his eyes, she answered in a muffled voice, "Fine." Her fingers fumbled over the tiny stitches as she worried that Adam would question why she was making a baby quilt.

"Did you go to town today?"

"I had lunch with Margo." That reminded her of the phone call she'd received from Mr. Dillby when she returned home, and she flushed, wishing Adam would stop watching her so closely. Did she have egg on her face?

"Is that right? And how is Margo?"

"She's just fine."

"I don't guess you've been to Stephenville lately?" he tossed out then, and despite his offhand tone, she was so startled she pricked her finger with her needle and cried out in pain. "Something wrong, Cammy?" he asked quickly.

She sucked the end of her finger and shook her head.

"Does that mean you haven't been to Stephenville?"

She frowned. "Do you mind if I go to Stephenville?"

"Not at all. I just thought maybe I should show more interest in your activities. You *are* my wife."

"I'm afraid my activities would bore you to tears." Even as she spoke gravely, Cammy's mouth twisted a little at the irony. What a time for him to get interested! Just when she couldn't confide in him.

That ended Adam's interrogation, but he continued to watch her unrelentingly until she finally excused herself and went to bed. She couldn't help hoping that his sudden husbandly concern would prompt him to resume his midnight visits, but she heard his car leave sometime after eleven, and she fell asleep still listening for his return.

Adam spent that night on the sofa in his office, after all. He took his shaving kit and a change of clothes with him, and he called the next day to tell Tally not to expect him for supper. "I'll come by for a shower late tonight," he said, late being the operative word. He wanted to make sure Cammy was already asleep when he arrived.

"Do you think that is wise?" Tally asked unexpectedly.

He curbed his impatience and said as gently as possible, "Yes, I do."

What he really wanted to do was rent an apartment, to get away from Cammy completely, so he wouldn't have to go home at all while she was there. If he had lived anywhere but Comanche, he would have done so, but no matter how alienated he felt from her, he refused to put Cammy through the gossip that would have resulted from his moving out. This wasn't her fault. She couldn't help it that she found it more difficult than she had first anticipated to live with a scarred-up monster. She couldn't help being willing to sell her inheritance to get out of the marriage.

His heart leaden and his throat strangely tight, Adam faced up to the fact that he had to stay out of Cammy's way. If that meant sleeping in his office for the next six months, he supposed he would get used to the idea. The uncomfortable sofa wasn't going to be nearly as hard to accept as the terrible emptiness of life without Cammy.

Cammy picked up her handbag from the car seat beside her and removed her compact to consult the small mirror. Her face looked perfect. So did her hair. She glanced down at the cotton knit chemise she wore. Cinched at the waist with a woven belt, and having a standaway neck and roll-up sleeves, the dress made her look capable and competent, she thought. And yet the peach color was soft and femininely flattering on her, especially with the matching leather pumps on her slim feet.

She reapplied a touch of peachy lip gloss, quickly checked the contents of her purse to be sure the checks were still there, and then breathed a panicky prayer. So much depended on the next few minutes! Her entire future—certainly her future with Adam—hung in the balance.

Swallowing hard, she climbed out of the red convertible and stood a moment with her hand on the car door after she slammed it shut. The top was up today, for although the October sun was bright, there was a bit of a nip in the air.

Time was passing swiftly. She and Adam had been married over three months now. She pressed a hand to her abdomen briefly as if to reassure herself that his baby was still growing there. Not that she showed yet; it was too early for that. But soon...soon Adam would have to know. She could already feel her body starting to change, and Adam might have discovered the changes if he had been at home, in bed with her where he belonged.

A bitter taste filled her mouth as Cammy wondered where Adam had been spending his nights for the past week. With April? Surely not! How could he, when Raleigh Magness was still alive, if not particularly well?

Cammy tried to push that question from her mind and think positive thoughts as she squared her shoulders and walked into the offices of Adam Neil, Attorney at Law. She had to believe Adam was an honorable man, that he would do the right thing today....

"Why, Cammy...hello!" Maggie said when she turned from her computer terminal and saw her boss's wife. "Adam didn't tell me you were coming in."

The secretary spoke louder than necessary, transmitting a subtle warning to Adam through his open office door. She didn't like the harried way he'd been looking lately, or the fact that he'd practically stopped going home altogether, and she suspected it had something to do with Cammy.

"He didn't know. Is he in?" Cammy heard a thump come from Adam's office, as if his feet had hit the floor, and grinned wryly at Maggie. "I guess that answers my question."

Just then he appeared in the doorway, his expression alert and wary, his short black hair disheveled as if nervous fingers had been plowing through it.

Cammy stared at him, thinking that she had never seen him so rumpled and tired-looking. His entire face was strained and pale, not just the scarred side. Even as she watched, he worked to straighten the knot in his tie and then combed both hands through his hair, smoothing it down into a semblance of order. His eyes held a guarded look that seemed to verge on hostility and made her heart contract with pain at what they had come to. She felt such respect for this man, and so much more!

"What can I do for you, Cammy?" he asked coolly.

She thought he sounded as if he had less concern for her affairs than he used to have when he was still just her lawyer. "Can you spare a few minutes of your time?" she asked, having little choice but to play along.

He shot a quick glance at Maggie, and Cammy wondered if he wanted his secretary to get him out of this. But Maggie only said, "It's after four o'clock, counselor. No more clients scheduled today, remember?"

Exhaling rather wearily, he made a visible effort to hide his disappointment and gestured for her to precede him. When she had seated herself on the sofa across from his desk, he closed the door to give them some privacy, then pulled a chair around and sat down facing her. "All right, Cammy. What brings you here?"

He made himself say it, even though he dreaded the answer. *This is it,* he was thinking. *She's ready to ask me for a divorce.*

Cammy forced herself not to look away from his gaze. She felt naked, as if he could see beneath her skin, while she couldn't read him at all. She could just sense his anger, his tension.

"There's something I have to ask of you," she began in as firm a voice as possible, praying it wouldn't start shaking. When Adam's mouth tightened, she realized he must resent the idea of granting her any more favors. "I know you've done enough for me already," she added quickly, continuing her carefully rehearsed speech. "You've been so kind and generous that I can never thank you enough, but there is one last thing that I have to do before I can get on with my life. I hope you understand."

Adam steeled himself to show no reaction. Her stiff words let him know she was prepared to go through with this no matter what he said. Admitting his love for her wasn't even an option; it certainly wouldn't stop her.

"I've sold Gran's farm to Billy Crenshaw," she was saying, looking braced for his disapproval. "I've got the checks with me, and I'm supposed to meet Lance, Joe Kenneth, and Babette at the café in half an hour. At that time I'm going to give them their money."

Since she seemed to be holding her breath for him to respond, he inclined his head. "Yes?" He sounded aloof and withdrawn as he waited for her to mention the divorce.

"I know you didn't want me to sell it," she hurried on, not knowing quite how to handle his lack of interest. Maybe he just didn't care anymore what she did. "I'm sorry if I've displeased you, Adam, but family is very, very important to me!" Tears sprang to her eyes and she blinked them away, thinking of the baby. "It matters more than the land...more than all the money in the world. My cousins may be the worst kind of jerks, but they're still my family, and I have to make some effort to fix whatever went wrong between us. I can't just keep being mad at them forever.''

Get to the point, he was thinking, his nerves stretching tauter by the second as he waited. Before he knew it, he had put it into words. ''What do you want from me, Cammy?''

''I want...I would like you to come with me when I meet Lance and the others, to give them their money.''

Adam sat very still, watching her blankly. ''You want me to go with you when you pay your cousins their money,'' he repeated as if to be quite sure he had heard her correctly.

''Yes. I know they've acted horrible to you. I know you have plenty of reason to hate them...''

He managed to nod, still struggling to process her request.

''...but I just think it's important for us to forgive them.'' She could barely see for the tears now. ''I've done things that need to be forgiven, Adam, and...well, maybe you have, too.'' The thought of April flickered across her mind, bringing a lump to her throat. She even had to forgive him for April! ''The Bible tells us that we can't hope to be forgiven unless we first forgive those who have hurt us. So I hoped...''

When her voice trailed off, he just sat staring at her, his face a stern mask to hide his racing thoughts. She might not be ready to ask for a divorce just yet, but she had disregarded his advice about selling the farm. And now she actually expected him to forgive that bastard. The one who had done his best to take advantage of Cammy's trusting innocence...who had mocked and slandered Adam, trampling his reputation and trying to make Cammy scorn him. And apparently Lance had succeeded in that. That was probably one reason Cammy was so determined to get a job and make a new life for herself.

As Adam's stony silence stretched, Cammy stood up. Her stomach churned with anguish at the realization that she had failed, with so much at stake. "I'm sorry," she whispered. "I guess that's too much to ask."

She turned and left his office, wretchedly aware of the raw, unguarded pain that she had glimpsed for just a second in his stormy eyes, the muscle twitching in his rigid jaw. He sat unmoving, not doing a thing to stop her.

Chapter Fourteen

"I'm sorry." Cammy apologized to each of her cousins as she handed them their portion of the money for Gran's farm. She spoke huskily, from the depths of a heart already half broken for love of Adam. "I never meant to hurt you."

The four Andersons occupied a corner table at the Continental Café. The last to arrive, Cammy had ordered coffee for everyone—which no one touched—and had taken the least favored seat, with her back to the door. Because there were customers already eating at the popular hangout, Cammy kept her voice low. From the corner of her eye, though, she could see other patrons glancing their way curiously.

Upon receiving his share, Joe Kenneth sent her a grin and muttered his thanks, while Babette merely sniffed. Lance narrowed his eyes to inspect his check, then gave her a calculating look as he folded and pocketed it. "So you realize you were wrong?"

Her shrug conveyed dejection. "As I said, I didn't mean to hurt anyone. I was just trying to plan for my future, the way Gran wanted me to do."

"You got some lousy advice," Lance said. "Another lawyer would have reminded you that you weren't the only heir involved, but I guess Adam Neil liked the idea of getting revenge."

Cammy started to tell Lance that she *had* consulted another lawyer—Sam Dillby—and that he had told her Adam's advice was excellent. But then she reminded herself that she was here to make peace, not to get more deeply embroiled in argument, so she let Lance's remark pass. Clasping her hands together, she forced a smile. "Anyway, the estate is settled now. I've forfeited my life estate and divided everything equally between the four of us. I hope we can put this behind us and...and just get on with our lives."

"You're still married to the smart-mouth attorney who caused all our trouble, aren't you?" Babette asked. "I don't know how you can expect us to forget the way he treated us."

"Adam didn't cause the trouble," Cammy said without thinking and saw displeasure flash across her cousin's face. *Careful,* she cautioned herself. She took a deep breath. "Look, folks, we're all that's left of the Anderson bloodline...all that's left of Gran and Grandpa. That ought to mean something. It ought to be enough to hold us together. Can't you forgive Adam for whatever you think he did to you? I've forgiven you—"

"You've forgiven us? Why, you self-righteous little prig!" Babette shrilled, causing heads to swivel, at the same time that Lance was snapping, "What we *think* he's done? I don't think, I know! He's always wanted to make me look bad, and it's just jealousy, pure and simple."

Cammy stiffened. "That's not true! Adam isn't jealous—"

"Adam has always been jealous," Lance cut in, loud enough for all the occupants of the dining room to hear him. "He hates everybody who looks better than him, which is ninety-nine percent of the population. If you weren't so gullible, you'd have realized that a long time ago. You wouldn't have thought you could change him by marrying him. It didn't work, did it? He's still the same... still bitter and mean enough to be capable of murdering his own brother just because a girl preferred Colby."

The café crowd gasped and then grew hushed at that. Flushing in dismay, Cammy wanted to turn around and tell everyone to mind their own business, but she couldn't blame them for eavesdropping. Her family wasn't exactly a model of discretion.

She opened her mouth to protest Lance's warped accusations, but her throat was too tight for speech. Babette took advantage of the silence to thrust out her chin and sneer, "We warned you you'd regret marrying a monster like Adam Neil. Considering what he did to his brother, it shouldn't surprise you what he tried to pull with us."

"Adam didn't hurt Colby," Cammy managed in a strangled whisper. She was so furious, she was shaking all over, yet she struggled to contain the anger.

"Oh, get off it, Cammy." Lance smiled a superior smile that she hated. "Everybody knows he did. You might as well admit you were wrong to feel sorry for him. After all, you wouldn't be here if you didn't want to make up to us. You said you want us to forgive you, right?''

Confusion swamped her as she looked at him, clouding her mind. It was true she had said she was sorry, but with every passing moment she was less sure that making peace with her cousins was the answer.

"Don't bother denying it. I heard you say so earlier." Lance crossed his arms. "If you really want to be one of us again, get rid of that jerk."

Cammy just kept staring, from Lance to Babette to Joe Kenneth, who looked as bewildered as she felt, and back to Lance. "Get rid of him?" she managed.

"You made a mistake when you married Adam Neil, but it's a mistake you can fix. Once you've divorced him, we can talk about maybe forgiving you and letting you be part of our family again. But not until then."

Suddenly the confusion cleared up and Cammy knew she'd heard enough. She shot to her feet while the rage boiled up inside her. *Calm down, Cammy,* she ordered herself, and then proceeded to ignore the order.

"I made a mistake all right, but it wasn't when I married Adam," she said through clenched teeth, her slender hands knotted at her sides. She wanted to take a swing at Lance and knock that smirk off his handsome, conceited face. She wanted to blacken one of Babette's beautiful blue eyes. Never in her life had she felt such a strong impulse to get violent, and the thing that had triggered it was her cousins' verbal attack on Adam. "My mistake was in thinking you people might care about anyone other than yourselves. You don't. You've forgotten everything our grandparents ever tried to teach us about love and loyalty. And somewhere along the line you've developed a sick, twisted, totally mistaken view of Adam Neil. I suspect it's a product of your own jealousy. You can't stand it that Adam grew up with money and we didn't."

Three startled faces gaped at Cammy from across the table. Total silence gripped the rest of the dining room. She knew everyone was listening, and all at once she was glad—glad for a chance to set the record straight.

"Let me just make one thing perfectly clear to you. I do not regret marrying Adam Neil. I have never regretted marrying him." She pressed both palms down on the table and leaned toward her cousins for emphasis. "Adam is a good man, a trustworthy man, probably the best man I know. He did not hurt his brother. Anybody in Comanche who doesn't know *that* is a fool and not worth bothering with. But even if he was a murderer, I still wouldn't regret marrying him." She shook her head fiercely, her eyes shooting blue sparks. "I'd marry him again in a minute, because I've been in love with that man since I was fourteen years old."

Straightening, she picked up her handbag from the chair and tucked it under one arm. "I know you think I'm old-fashioned, and you're right about that. Family matters to me in a way you'll never understand. As for my being part of your family again, that's up to you. At the moment, I'm more concerned with being part of Adam's family."

It was just brave talk. She wasn't really a part of Adam's family, and never had been. Cammy acknowledged that as she turned to go, but she kept her chin up anyway out of sheer defiance.

She took two steps toward the entry and halted when she saw the man standing just inside, watching her.

"Adam!" she gulped. How long had he been there? How much had he heard?

When it became apparent that she wouldn't—or couldn't—move, he approached her. The rest of the world waited in fascination as Adam came face-to-face with Cammy. He stared down at her, and she stared back, swallowing nervously, feeling her defiance fizzle.

It wasn't so much his stunned expression that shook her as it was the flame in his eyes. A flame of hope. Of bare longing. A burning question that she could read almost as plainly as if he were speaking the words aloud: *Do you mean what you just said, Cammy?*

She drew in a deep unsteady breath. Then, ignoring everyone else in the room, she curved her palm against his jaw. "Yes," she said softly, answering his unspoken inquiry. Stretching, she touched her mouth to his and whispered against his lips, "Yes, Adam."

Without sparing a glance for anyone else, they turned to the door. Adam laced his fingers through Cammy's, and they walked outside into the cool sunshine.

It seemed that there was so much to be said, and at the same time so little need for words!

They left Adam's car at the café and drove home in Cammy's. Halfway to the Neil place he murmured out of the blue, still sounding dazed, "You've really never regretted it?" He kept his eyes fixed on the road as he waited for her answer, which came at once.

"Never. Not for a minute." She paused a couple of heartbeats, then said, "Are you angry that I sold the farm?"

Unable to speak, he shook his head. If she hadn't sold the land, he wouldn't have overheard her stand up for him in a way nobody in town had ever done before. Nobody, that is, except for maybe Louella Anderson.

When they arrived home and walked in together, Tally took one look at them and announced that she wanted the rest of the evening off to go to a movie. One eyebrow raised in quizzical amazement, Adam started to point out that Tally had never in her life gone to a movie, but instead he found himself telling her to have a good time.

"Before I forget, miss," Talese said on her way out the door, "your cousin called a few minutes ago. He wants you to come to Sunday dinner at his house."

She frowned at that. "Lance? He wants just me?"

"Not Lance, the younger one. He wants you and your husband to come." And Tally disappeared, shutting the door behind her.

Adam produced a crooked grin. "Do I detect a white flag waving?"

Cammy's expression was softening, too. "I wouldn't be surprised. Joe Kenneth never could hold a grudge." She wasn't so sure about the others.

For a moment Adam stood silent, remembering what Cammy had said, first to him at his office, then to her cousins. Family was important. So was forgiving. Hesitantly he said, "Would you like to accept his invitation?"

She nearly smiled, hearing his cautious *I'll go if you will* tone. She wanted to accept, all right. More than anything, she wanted her family to accept Adam. But what if Adam couldn't handle the news she had for him? What if she was misreading him?

"I'll call Joe Kenneth tomorrow and give him our answer," she said. By tomorrow she should know how Adam really felt.

They ate the supper Tally had already prepared, then cleaned up the kitchen. A subtle constraint was starting to sharpen the air between them, and Cammy realized that perhaps they had more to talk about than she had thought.

Part of the tension she attributed to the weeks that had passed since Adam had touched her. Being close enough, like this, to inhale his delicious musky scent made her exquisitely aware of how much she'd needed him. Somehow she knew he was feeling it keenly, too. The way he wrenched his eyes away when they strayed below her chin...his white-knuckled grip on whatever his hands happened to be holding...the tremor that shuddered through him when they inadvertently brushed against each other in the kitchen doorway...his swiftly smothered groan...

"Cammy, I want—" He broke off and looked away. Finally he met her gaze again, his eyes shuttered. "At the café you told your cousins you have loved me since you were fourteen." His brow furrowed. "Why would you say something like that?"

"Because it's the truth."

"The truth? How can it be?" He sounded puzzled, torn apart by the question. "When you were fourteen, I was almost twice your age."

She rolled her eyes. "Absolutely ancient!"

"Besides, my scars—"

"Adam," she interrupted him, catching his hand as it rose toward his cheek. She brought it to her mouth and whispered a kiss across the palm, her eyes full of love. "Your scars aren't important. They never mattered at all."

Grunting, he pulled back. "I wish I could believe you, but you must have forgotten...I saw you that morning in the bathroom." He turned away from her and stood at the kitchen window, his back straight and his shoulders stiff. "That was exactly what I expected to happen if I ever fell in love." His words, so full of precious meaning to her, were flat. "That's why I fought against it—why I never stayed around until the sun came up. My face is bad enough, but the rest . . . I knew the scars would turn you off."

"There is nothing wrong with your face," Cammy began, but she saw from the proud way his head went up that he wasn't buying it. Her heart plunged. She couldn't let him go on thinking that! "Adam, your scars had nothing to do with making me sick that day," she insisted, groping for words. "My stomach was . . . was just upset."

"It's okay, Cammy." He slowly turned back around, his expression fixed. "I understand."

"No, you don't understand," she muttered. "And you don't believe me, either. That hurts!"

"I'm sorry," he said, unwilling to lie and pretend to believe her.

A gleam suddenly appeared in her eyes. "A minute ago you started to say you wanted me. Didn't you?"

Adam thrust his hands into his pockets and squared his shoulders, struggling to control his own tumultuous feelings. "Don't worry about me. I'll get over it."

Slanting an impishly provocative smile at him, she moved to his side and tucked her hand through his arm. "Come on." She started in the direction of the bedrooms. "Let's get over it together."

He went reluctantly, tugged along by his enthusiastic wife. "Cammy, I don't want—"

"Yes, you do. And so do I!"

Something made her lead him to his own bedroom. Once inside, with lamplight falling on the wedding-ring quilt and the door shutting out the rest of the world, she released his arm. Then she began to undress with an unhurried, unconsciously seductive grace that held him silent and entranced until she stood before him naked.

"Oh, Lord," he sighed raggedly when she had finished. He shut his eyes to block out her irresistible image and shook his head, as if that would stop the heat of love and need from sweeping through him. "Please don't..."

She came close to him and undid his necktie, then started to unbutton his shirt. When her bare thighs brushed his, she swallowed audibly but kept working her way down his chest toward his belt buckle.

"Cammy, *please!*" In a purely reflexive move, his hands spanned her waist and tightened there, dragging her against him just as she unzipped his pants. He buried his face in her hair, his lips nuzzling behind her ear and his heart flipping over. "Please don't pretend with me!"

Somehow she managed to work his shirt off his tautly muscled shoulders without separating from his warmth. She kissed his throat, letting her breath tantalize his skin, and felt him shiver. "I've never had to pretend with you. That's what comes from having loved you since I was a kid." Looping her arms around his neck, she stretched against him like a supple, sexy cat. "I adore everything about you."

Adam held himself rigid for a second longer, then felt the last of his resistance melt in the glow of sweet desire that pulsed through him. Ripping off his shoes and socks and stepping out of his trousers, he lifted Cammy onto the middle of his bed. Driven by the tender ache in his heart, he wrapped himself around her, forgetting that he'd left the light on. Forgetting to worry whether there was anything about his body that would turn her off. Forgetting everything except the fragrant, eagerly responsive woman in his arms.

Her hands trailed over his back, his hips, his legs, tracing the fire-brands and loving him anyway. Dear Lord, she loved him so much! Cammy sighed his name as she arched against him, and her mouth met his in a slow soft kiss that told of infinite emotion.

Coaxed ever closer to him by that magical kiss, she lost herself in Adam, and he in her. Their lovemaking carried them to new heights and set them adrift in places meant for dreams and happy endings. Tenderness spun a warm, golden cocoon around them both.

Later, Adam lay watching in fascination as Cammy's hands still caressed him, telling him she couldn't get enough. He shook his head. "I'm not sure I understand you."

She shrugged lazily. "What's there to understand? Gran always said you were the handsomest man in ten counties, and I grew up believing her. I can see now that she wanted me to marry you."

When he choked out a gruff laugh, she looked up and saw something suspiciously bright glinting in his eyes. "I still don't understand, but thank God for your grandmother!"

Cammy was silently agreeing with Adam when he grew solemn and cupped his hand around her nape. "Cammy, I want you to move back into this bedroom, this time for keeps. Will you do that?"

A lump of painful need formed in her throat. What she would give to do just that, no questions asked! She could never deny loving him, but she also couldn't share him any longer. "What about April?" she asked tautly.

"April? April Magness? I'm not sure what—" He stopped, an uneasy frown twitching over his features.

"Don't say that, Adam." Her eyes were big, hurt. "I saw the ring she gave you. I saw the engraved message."

"Love, April?" That dear, familiar, wry half smile transformed his face once more. Before she could kill him for making light of this, he held up his free hand to show her. "I'm not wearing the ring. I've never worn it."

"But you kept it."

"I kept it in the hopes that maybe she would finally decide she'd paid her debt to me. And it seems to have worked. She hasn't come around to apologize again."

"Apologize for what?" Cammy asked blankly.

"She thinks my scars are her fault. She thinks it was her fault that Colby tried to kill me."

Understanding dawned on Cammy. "Because April got a crush on you, and Colby went off the deep end about it?"

Years of anguish showed in his eyes as he nodded. "This is some family you've married into, Camelia."

"Listen, Adam, don't go holding the Neils responsible for what Colby did." She shook a finger in his face, only inches from her own. "And don't you blame me for what my cousins did. For the most part, the Andersons *and* the Neils have been a pretty upstanding bunch." A thoughtful expression took over her features and she ran one teasing fingertip down his chest. "Have you ever wondered what we'd come up with if we combined our families? If we, you know, sort of crossbred the Neils and Andersons?"

"Crossbred?" His mouth quirked with humor at the term, then straightened as her meaning registered. He grew very still, and she became aware that one of his taut hands lay on her slightly swollen belly. After a moment he demanded, "What are you telling me?"

Was that dread making his voice shake? She was feeling
rather panicky herself. "What I'm *trying* to tell you..
what I've been trying to figure out how to tell you for
ages...is that you're going to be a father, Adam."

He let out his breath sharply, and his hand moved to cup
her breast, gently weighing the fullness, the heaviness of it.
"I knew there was a difference," he whispered, turning
and cradling her in his strong arms.

"After all, you never asked if I was using birth control."

"No, I never asked." He spoke roughly, hoarsely, and
when Cammy pulled back to look at him, there was no
mistaking the sparkle of tears in his eyes this time. He gave
a long, slow head shake. "A baby!" It would take some
getting used to.

His awe-stricken tone reassured her, but she asked anyway, "You don't mind?"

"Mind? Oh, angel...I suppose I started hoping you'd
have my child as soon as I realized I'd fallen in love with
you." Adam stroked her stomach with trembling fingers.
"But I couldn't admit that even to myself, until just now.
I thought I'd never be part of a family again. I almost
convinced myself I didn't want to be—"

"But you do want that?"

Turning his dark head, he gave her a level look...a look
of such intense and concentrated love that Cammy felt it
tingle right down to her toes. "Oh, yes," he murmured.
"Don't ever doubt that." He shook his head again.
"Thank God I didn't let my stupid pride and stubbornness keep me from following you to the café today!"

"Do you think you can forgive my cousins, Adam?"

"I think I have to," he said after a moment, sounding
pensive. "No matter how they feel about me, I don't want

our family to start out full of hate. From experience I can tell you, that's a slow but sure way to die. I want our family to be founded on love."

Our family. It had a beautiful ring to it. And speaking of rings ...

"We're going shopping," Cammy announced abruptly. "First thing tomorrow."

"I thought you didn't like shopping."

"Oh, I can take it or leave it." Lifting his hand between them, she held it against her cheek. "But our beautiful baby is going to need some things. You need some comfortable, short-sleeved shirts...maybe some shorts to wear around here." He seemed on the verge of interrupting, so she hurried on. "And it's time I bought you a wedding ring. From now on I want to be sure everybody knows you're a married man." She brushed her lips across the back of his fingers. "Will you wear my ring?"

He studied the hand she was kissing so softly, and it was as if he had never seen it before. His heart melted a little more at each of those tenderly evocative kisses. For the first time, deep inside, he felt the truth of what she had told him: The scars really didn't matter. They didn't matter because with love in her eyes, she no longer even saw them.

A warm sea of contentment engulfed Adam as he caught her chin and tipped her face up a couple of inches. "I'll wear your ring, Mrs. Neil. As long as I have breath in me, I'll wear it."

"As long as you have breath, hmm?" She eyed him with exaggerated concern. "Gosh, I hope you'll be good for another few years. Now that you mention it, you *are* pretty old—"

His mouth covered hers and cut short her sassy observation. Hours later, he was still busy demonstrating how wrong she was.

*   *   *   *   *

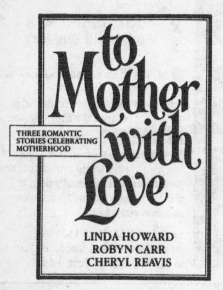
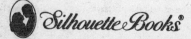

 **Silhouette Books®**

SILHOUETTE BOOKS ARE NOW AVAILABLE IN STORES AT THESE CONVENIENT TIMES EACH MONTH*

Silhouette Desire and Silhouette Romance

> May titles: April 10
> June titles: May 8
> July titles: June 5
> August titles: July 10

Silhouette Intimate Moments and Silhouette Special Edition

> May titles: April 24
> June titles: May 22
> July titles: June 19
> August titles: July 24

We hope this new schedule is convenient for you. With only two trips each month to your local bookseller, you will always be sure not to miss any of your favorite authors!

Happy reading!

Please note: There may be slight variations in on-sale dates in your area due to differences in shipping and handling.

*Applicable to U.S. only.

SDATES-RR

Take 4 bestselling love stories FREE

Plus get a FREE surprise gift!

Special Limited-time Offer

Silhouette Reader Service®

Mail to
In the U.S.
3010 Walden Avenue
P.O. Box 1867
Buffalo, N.Y. 14269-1867

In Canada
P.O. Box 609
Fort Erie, Ontario
L2A 5X3

YES! Please send me 4 free Silhouette Romance® novels and my free surprise gift. Then send me 6 brand-new novels every month, which I will receive months before they appear in bookstores. Bill me at the low price of $2.25* each. There are no shipping, handling or other hidden costs. I understand that accepting the books and gift places me under no obligation ever to buy any books. I can always return a shipment and cancel at any time. Even if I never buy another book from Silhouette, the 4 free books and the surprise gift are mine to keep forever.

*Offer slightly different in Canada—$2.25 per book plus 69¢ per shipment for delivery. Sales tax applicable in N.Y. Canadian residents add applicable federal and provincial sales tax.

215 BPA HAYY (US)   315 BPA 8176 (CAN)

Name   (PLEASE PRINT)

Address   Apt. No.

City   State/Prov.   Zip/Postal Code

This offer is limited to one order per household and not valid to present Silhouette Romance® subscribers. Terms and prices are subject to change.

SROM-8PADR   © 1990 Harlequin Enterprises Limited

Bestselling author NORA ROBERTS captures all the
romance, adventure, passion and excitement of Silhouette in
a special miniseries.

THE CALHOUN WOMEN

Four charming, beautiful and fiercely independent
sisters set out on a search for a missing family
heirloom—an emerald necklace—and each finds
something even more precious... passionate romance.

Look for THE CALHOUN WOMEN miniseries
starting in June.

COURTING CATHERINE
Silhouette Romance #801

July
A MAN FOR AMANDA
Silhouette Desire #649

August
FOR THE LOVE OF LILAH
Silhouette Special Edition #685

September
SUZANNA'S SURRENDER
Silhouette Intimate Moments #397

CALWOM-1